I0714539

Published by: Cinnabar Moth Publishing LLC
Santa Fe, New Mexico

Cover Design by: Ira Geneve

ISBN-13: 978-1-953971-66-1
Library of Congress Control Number: 2022946918

Icarus over Collins

HECTOR DUARTE JR.

Bailey Cohen

There he is. Sandy Mangual doing his acrobatics high above Collins Avenue. Eleven stories up. Again. How many goddam times are me and his mom going to have to talk to him? He's gotten good at swinging like a pendulum; one, two, then at the peak of the third swing, swoosh. Releasing his grip and landing on the balcony like someone out of Cirque du Soleil.

Behind me, Gabe says, "That kid's going to slip one day and bye bye, birdie."

I was so entranced by Sandy, I hadn't even heard him. "I'll call Ximena later."

"Couldn't wait till dinner?" he says, tapping my glass.

"Just warming up before the girls get here."

"They're coming over again? It's only Tuesday, and the three of you are partying like it's a forever weekend. Some of us work tomorrow."

"Wear the noise cancellers I bought you."

"That's not the point."

Sandy is still out on the balcony, patting down his jeans and checking himself before going inside. I yell across Collins at the top of my lungs. "I'm telling your mom."

"He can't hear you, Bailey."

Of course he can't. With the distance and constant honking traffic beneath us.

I mirror Sandy as he steps back inside, closes the hurricane-impact sliding-glass door behind him.

"He's got balls dangling like that," I whisper.

"Until the day he doesn't. More importantly. I don't want your friends coming over tonight." Gabe pulls the glass from my hand. "You have to control this shit." He swallows it down hard enough I hear the gulp and makes to the kitchen.

"Come on, party pooper. Remember when we used to party all the time, party all the time, party all the tie-ime?"

He stops but does not turn toward me. "Yeah, back when you still worked full tie-ime."

What a dick. He keeps walking so I jog up behind him, scoop his feet out from under. He hits the floor like an anvil. Since high school, I've been doing this shit to people and it's never worked before. I mean, he drops so hard, I laugh. A nervous laugh, because I have no idea what else to do. Gabe does not like to be laughed at.

He grabs the glass that miraculously did not shatter. "Go ahead; do what you do best. Ignore the issue completely. I'm going to be in my room and you three better not wake me or I'm kicking all of your drunk asses out of here. I swear to God."

I turn and stare again across at the balcony where minutes earlier a sixteen-year-old dangled high over Miami Beach. I get close enough to place my palms against the hurricane-impact windows. I'm doing this as a meditative exercise. To avoid going off on Gabe.

All right. So, I don't work a full-time job that requires an eight-hour grind. Sure, I like to drink. More than most, maybe. But I'm up every morning to meet clients. Okay, client, singular, which doesn't bring in a full-time income. Yet. But it will. A year and a half back, Gabe swore up and down he was fine with it as long as I chipped in whatever possible for utilities, cooked, and kept the house clean. None of his self-righteousness about it back then. A lot happens in a year.

This place is too amazing not to show off. It keeps me calm. All I have to do is walk outside, listen to the waves crash, the cars honking, smell the salty air, watch the waning dusk make tall torches out of the light posts snaking their way north on Collins and up through Sunny Isles. Worlds apart: a year back inside that matchbox-sized efficiency way out West in Miccousoukee Country, wondering what the fuck a bachelor's degree in physical therapy was good for. I swore then I'd show off a place like this if I could. Now that I can, why not?

The girls are surprised I put up with it. There's an ulterior motive. Gabe's so fucking hot and his parents own the place, so he barely has to work for this high-rise condo with a view of the ocean out one panoramic window and a lengthy expanse of Collins out the other. No more tiny studio that requires walking through the bathroom to get to my bed. I can afford a wine bottle a night. That was a dream one year back. Now it's reality, and I'm celebrating because Bailey Cohen is all grown up.

I'm half a bottle in while Clarissa and Hanna are still at a glass and a half. They've been nursing the whole night, petrified to wake Gabe. Constantly shushing and whispering at me to keep it down, pointing at the wall dividing us from him. Loving how scared they are, I ramp up the ante with some music. Who better to complement a drinking session than Amy Winehouse?

Her nighttime Glastonbury set. I've got every beautiful stumble, mumble, and drunken rant memorized.

It's funny to watch the girls inch their ways toward leaning, forcing arm stretches and fake yawns. I crank it up just when Amy punches an eager fan who reaches for the mic.

"Turn it d—" Hannah starts.

Before she can finish, Gabe's in his rumpled PJs, bleary-eyed, leaning a tight fist against the drywall. "Will you shut that fucking shit off?"

Clarissa tilts her head toward the door, signaling Hanna. "We'd better—"

"Don't fucking move. You two have been needing to hear this for a minute," Gabe says.

I stand between them. "Don't talk to them like that."

He smirks and turns to me. It's a smile like he's been waiting for this, some time coming. "Know what, Jane fucking Fonda? Keep drinking like this. Watch what happens when your metabolism catches up to you." He turns back to the girls. "And you two cunts."

The wine bottle shatters just under his fist, splashing the wall and his pajama bottoms purple. I purposely missed. Believe me, had I wanted to, I could have sliced it across his temple. Had a right mind to.

Gabe tightens his fists and lunges after us. I yell at them to run, keeping caboose until we get to the door, and I slam it behind him.

Gabe's fist pounds against the door like a jack hammer. "Don't come back up here. Any of you."

I pound back, because fuck him.

Hanna and Clarissa take off.

There is no noise from inside. Looking down at the door crack, I see when he snaps off the light.

His patience is thinning. Last time, he dumped all my booze down the drain, and I promised never to do it again. By the end of the week, I'd found a reason to celebrate and tip a glass again; he didn't complain when I told him I had a new client: Ximena Mangual, the prominent telenovela actress who lives across the street, mother of Sandy Mangual.

Fifteen minutes pass. That asshole locked me out. I keep things civil and knock again; nothing. In seconds, my phone chimes. *You're not sleeping here tonight. Figure it out, guapa.*

I lose it and start banging on the door, yelling at him not to be such a selfish motherfucker. I mean, I'm really trying to kick through.

Sheldon, the next-door neighbor, peeks his head out. "Don't you two work? I'm trying to get some goddam sleep in here. Don't make me call front desk and have security come up here for whatever domestic dispute you two got going on again."

"Mind your own fucking business, maricon de mierda!"

Sheldon shakes his head and gently closes the door.

I go down before security comes up.

Bernardo Castillo is waiting for the elevator when I get to the lobby. It's not the first time he's been called up there for a Bailey–Gabe row. "¿Todo bien? I was just—" he starts.

"I know. We had another argument. He kicked me out. Can I stay down here tonight?"

"You know that's not—"

Bernardo is not just security. He's the building's jack-of-all trades: maintenance, front desk on long weekends. I've even seen him valeting cars. Lately, security's sent him to intervene during mine and Gabe's dramatic fallouts. They must've noticed we're close.

"Please. I wouldn't ask if I had anywhere else to go. Te lo ruego. Por favor."

"Bailey. No puedes seguir en esto." Bernardo looks back at Mister Schecter eyeballing us from behind front desk. "Promise me you'll move around. You can't stay in one place or me pelan el culo."

"I'll stay down here and make some calls."

"Perfect."

I walk around the lobby and phone the girls. Hannah answers that they found a nearby bar and are partying it up without drama.

Just when I think I've got no place to stay, Bernardo comes back pissed and offers for me to spend the night. Not in the way it sounds. I know that right off. If not, I'd have not taken the offer. Bernardo's a good guy and I'm grateful. I make sure to let him know by buying a case of beer and having our own happy hour until late in the evening.

Before dozing off for a few hours of sleep, I text Gabe. *No worries, found a place to stay. I'll come pick my shit up this weekend.* I complement the message with a shot of the empty beer bottles on the coffee table, because fuck him.

When I wake up the next morning, he's written back. *Be out by tomorrow and slide the key under the door when you're done.*

Me and Bernardo walk back into Las Brisas together and, as inconspicuous as we try to be, Schecter spots us coming into the lobby through the service entrance and immediately waves Bernardo over. I'm hoping I don't cost this guy his job and already have a confrontation with Schecter up my sleeve in case it comes to that.

I get to Gabe's door and there's a note taped there, written in his chicken-scratch scrawl: WORKING EARLY. SHIFT ENDS ABOUT 2. BE GONE BY THEN!

Fucking dickhead. It's better we don't get to see one another because we might just make evening news headlines.

I'll enjoy his place one last time. After coffee percolates, I sit by the window, staring at the expanse of all the beautiful blue water lapping Miami's sandy shore. A little girl runs away from the water, back toward it, away from it again. Traffic snakes its way through Collins and out to the mainland. So much going on out there. Something about all that action going on without me tells me it's time to cut out on my own. This needs to happen this way.

That sentiment relaxes me enough to roll a joint I plan on smoking on Gabe's couch, in the middle of the living room, because fuck him. As I'm licking the end shut, my cellphone alarm rings.

Shit. Ximena Mangual's session. In the craziness and drama that's been life the last twenty-four hours, I'd forgotten about my one client, the one who's going to help me build up the clientele list. Can't let this big fish get away. Unless I want to be one of the schlubs sitting in traffic, honking their way to a nine-a.m. shift. Time to exercise the frustration away.

Geared up, I get to Ximena's condo across the street and run the thirteen flights up to Ximena's floor.

Sandy answers with a huge, sneaky smile on his face, backpack slung across one shoulder, hair wet and tousled. "Hey, Bay."

"Hey, San."

"Um. . . Mom's not here."

I deflate.

"Fuck. She didn't call you? They told her last night she had to be in for an early shoot. Sorry, man. I'll tell her to pay you double next session."

"It's cool. Just tell her to let me know when she wants me to come back around."

"Yup."

I wedge my foot in the door before he shuts it. "Hey, don't forget I see you from my window. Stop jumping down from the top balcony."

"I'm sixteen. Mom doesn't want to make me a copy of the key till I'm seventeen—one week—so until then. . ."

"Risk your life pretending to be Cliffhanger?"

"What's that?"

"A movie with Sylvester Stallone."

"Who?"

"Stop jumping down is all."

"I leave the balcony door open, come and go as I please. Devon upstairs lets me jump down. What's the whoop?"

He makes to close the door again. I push it with my fist this time. "Seriously, man. Stop fucking around or I'll tell her."

With three conjoined fingers in the air, he pledges scout's honor. I've lied plenty myself. I know he's blowing smoke, which I'll be doing momentarily in the middle of Gabe's beautiful, beach-view condo.

I descend the stairs at a dead run. Outside the Landings, I look across the street and up at our condo, Brisas Canarias. God damn, it's going to be a bitch making a lateral move from a place like this but it's better than being walled inside a luxury prison.

In a couple hours, all my shit is packed, Gabe's living room smells like the lot at a Phish show, and to really smoke him out, I've made curry chicken for lunch. There's a sweet satisfaction knowing it's going to take him days of opening the windows to get the smell out. The one time I made curry, he didn't stop bitching about the smell still being in his nostrils and his stomach being ripped to shit. For such a professed man, he sure is a capital-P pussy.

Right on time, my stuff is packed, head is swimming, belly is full, and the condo smells of petty revenge and harbored anger. Perfect. I walk to the glass windows to look out and finish the roach. Truth is, I'm going to massively miss this view.

I walk out to the balcony and hit the pungent roach to Miami Beach's soundtrack. Waves crashing on one side, cars honking on the other, both blend into a meditative rhythm that helps anchor me to my situation. There's a lapse between the sight of waves and the sound of their crashing that's addicting. Nature's deliberate pause, forcing me to wait just momentarily enough, for the full sensory experience. Lungs fill with salty air as I inhale. Squeezing tightly on the rail, I close my eyes and just listen. Projecting the image of crashing waves I've just seen to the back of my eyelids. With every inhalation, I envision flecks of sea salt entering through my nostrils and settling everywhere stress and pain exist. I exhale. Much better.

My eyes open to see that slippery fucker Sandy at it again. He and Devon out on the balcony, passing a joint between them, laughing, high-fiving, hugging it out.

Ximena's going to hear about what her sneaky son is up to. I turn right, looking out to the ocean. A kite surfer cuts into a wave, is airborne for what feels like minutes, and glides back down onto the water.

Across the street, the sound of shattering glass rips me from my daydream. High above The Landings, Sandy dangles over Collins Avenue.

Glass rains to the street below.

"Get back up!" I scream like he can hear me. Like those words could magically catapult him back to stability and safety. Sixteen fucking years old. Too impatient to wait seven days for a

God damn key.

Sandy falls fast to the ground. He is not suspended like the kite surfer, is instead pulled to the concrete below. I remember Gabe's words. Repeated so often, they've become a mantra. "Bye bye, birdie."

Fixated, I follow his young body's trajectory straight to the pavement, fast as a missile. Pedestrians down below point and follow his track, too. A couple of silent, harrowing seconds after he hits, a small crowd surrounds the body. Seconds after that, screams reach my ears.

Bernardo Castillo

Me han agotado. And it's only Wednesday. More than a year working at Brisas Canarias and I'm finally coming to understand the eccentricities of these gringos. Understanding there's no pattern to it, because these rich people live a vacation all the time their entire lives. Like tonight. There's no long weekend. No Jewish holiday. It's just the beginning of summer and you'd think it was maldito Cuatro de Julio. Americans really love to celebrate their independence day. All day long with the explosions popping off all over the city. I don't get it. Back home, you hear that many explosions, you go inside.

That anxiety was the reason que me fui de mi bello Cuba in the first place. Bueno, that and Eugenia. I didn't come to the United States to live like I did back there. I did not leave her behind in vain.

I like the job at Las Brisas; off the books and pays cash, decent cash compared with a lot of people I know working wineries in The Redlands that pay the daily equivalent of a Taco Bell combo meal.

Compared to that, this place is a country club, aunque joden bastante estos gringos. My official title is *Maintenance Specialist*. That doesn't stop Schecter from putting me behind the front desk, the valet podium, pressure-washing the sidewalks around the building. Wherever someone is needed, Bernardo, the jack-of-all-trades, fills the void.

Tonight, I'm in the lobby working security because el muy vago head of security Nestor, who's so fat he couldn't chase a tortoise, called in at the last minute saying he thinks he might be coming down with flu. And the lobby is jammed. I offered to work concierge because I'm a damn machine under pressure. Schecter, el jefe, the control freak, told me to control the lobby. They needed a managerial face at concierge. Whatever that's supposed to mean, el muy resingado.

What's the appeal of Miami Beach? Paying through the nose to live on an island choked by putrid exhaust fumes farted out by rich peoples' cars, trapped by water on all sides, constant traffic, and AirBnB guests for neighbors. No thank you. Que se lo metan por el ojo del culo.

On this first day of June, the lobby is jammed with visitors and AirBnB check-ins. A good amount look like they just graduated high school—young. The rest are botoxed viejos crop-dusting their over-perfumed designer smells at the expense of everyone else's breathing comfort.

Five hours into shift and I haven't stopped once. Descansaré cuando me muera.

But, my heart's racing, my chest tightens. The pattern is familiar now and I know what to do to calmarme. Esta mierda never happened back home. The gift of democracy came with anxiety attacks I'd never experienced until I'd crossed into American airspace. A duty-free gift I never asked for.

"Castillo," Mister Schecter shouts from behind the

concierge desk, waving me over. "Sheldon de Paz called. Cohen and her boyfriend are at it again. Check it out, make sure they're not killing each other."

An older lady waiting at the desk clears her throat, and Mister Schecter profusely apologizes for not having seen her.

On the way up, I practice my speech to Bailey Cohen. Me cae bien Bailey. She gets a bad rap for mooching off el ricachón de su novio, Gabe Acevedo, who only stays in the condo because his parents own it. He works at Mount Sinai to establish independence from his parents. Bailey says it's all bullshit. The moment he needs anything, he runs like an antelope to mom, the human ATM.

We run into each other at least once a week. More, if they fight. Bailey loves to speak in Spanish y se defiende bastante bien. I like practicing my English. I know it's way more broken and sloppier than she lets on. La verdad es que Bailey Cohen is the only friend I have en estos Estados Unidos.

I take in slow, deep breaths to fill my chest as he waits for the next elevator cart. Fucking Gabe Acevedo es tremendo ma—

"Bernardo." Bailey smiles.

"Que pasa, Bailey? Schecter sent me up. Everything okay?"

"No, no hace falta. Please, look. Gabe and me had a bad one tonight." Bailey motions to one of the couches in the lobby.

I have to go up because Sheldon is a tenant and, technically, Bailey isn't. Schecter is still busy with the older lady who heard him curse. With a quick crane of my neck, I motion Bailey to the couch at the far end of the lobby, a blind spot from concierge.

Bailey pregunta si puede pasar la noche.

Ni modo, I tell her. If she's caught, me pelan el culo.

Bailey says she has no place to go. Reminds me how Gabe is and promises he'll get over it by tomorrow. Please. She has nowhere else to go.

Me cago en la suerte. What am I supposed to do? Let the girl pasar la noche God knows where in these Miami streets?

"Wait here. I have to go check on Mister Sheldon. No te vayas," I tell her.

There's no response at Sheldon's door y no voy a esperar mucho. Soon as I turn back toward the elevator, el viejo amargado opens his door and snaps, "Go away. I'm trying to get some goddam sleep. I pay rent here for peace, not stress."

¿Puedes creer al muy hijo de puta?

Down in the lobby, Bailey's donde le dije que se escondiera. At the back corner, pacing and talking on her phone. Mas vale no sea con Gabe.

She waves at me, and I'm about to walk over there when Schecter's piercing whistle rings across the lobby. Odio cuando me llama como un perro. But it's better than working soft taco wages.

"All good with the Sheldon situation?" Schecter asks.

"Went upstairs, said he didn't want to be bothered."

"Bien. Go home, Castillo, you've earned it. Thank you for all that you do."

"I'm supposed to work a full shift tonight. You're rammed."

"If you must know, Nestor called and said he's feeling better."

"Go home, Castillo. Unless you don't want to work a full shift tomorrow."

Que so maricon. What kind of sense does that make? ¿Sabes porque? Porque Nestor speaks the language and tiene sus papeles al dia.

Bailey's still on the phone, only now she's sitting on the couch. I hang back and let her finish.

She pulls the phone from her ear. "This is bullshit. I just

want Schecter to think I'm busy so he doesn't kick me out."

"¿Que paso?" I ask.

"Gabe es un maricon egoísta. ¿Pero ya tu lo sabias, no?

I have to laugh.

I think about it for a second because what I'm going to offer could become tremendo lio, but I can't help myself. Eugenia siempre decia I loved playing with fire.

"Oye, Schecter just told me I had to go home for the night. ¿Quieres pasar la noche en mi casa?" Sounds so goddam wrong. "I mean, just to sleep obviously. I have to come back early tomorrow. I'll bring you right back."

"Si no te conociera bien, Bernardo Castillo, I'd swear you were trying to. . ."

I look back and see Schecter eyeballing us.

"Mira, I need to go but if your answer is yes, I park on the second floor of the garage. I'll wait twenty minutes. If you're not there by then, adios, muy buenas."

"I'll give you my answer right now." She stands to leave.

"Nope. You need to wait. If Schecter sees me, me. . .

"¿Pela el culo?"

"Precisely. Give me five minutes."

Bailey tiene buenos modales. On the way home, we stop at a gas station where she loads up on beer and snacks. "You're not sleeping tonight," she promises me.

Cuando llegamos a mi pequeño efficiency I can't tell if she's being sarcastic when she looks around and marvels at how cool a place it is. It's the best I can do given my income and Miami rent rates. Mi pequeño domicilio queda donde Little Havana grazes

Downtown. Tucked behind a bigger house, you'd never know it's there unless I told you, and that's just the way I like it.

Se tira en el sofa, takes her shoes off. "Pasame una cerveza y ven para aca," she says, slapping the empty space next to her.

And so the night goes. The first time, en estos Estados Unidos, I've spent hours alone with someone, hablando mierda, pasando rato, not even stressing the fact I have to be at work tomorrow for the 7 a.m. shift. Pa' su madre.

Within three hours, we've killed the twelve pack between us. Mira que esa niña puede tomar.

Says she's glad things played out like they did. She needs to get out of there and is going to be gone by the time Gabriel blinks. How sad he's going to be without her.

¿Sabes cuando alguien toma demasiado and they just start pouring out every single thing that's wrong and needs fixing in their life? That's pretty much the type of session we had. I was glad to listen. Coño, I was just glad to have someone over the house.

Y no. No terminamos en la cama, para nada. When the beer was done, I told her to go into my room and I'd sleep on the couch. When she insisted the other way, I didn't push it, and remind her we needed to be up early tomorrow.

I pop two aspirin.

"Those things destroy your liver," she says.

"Buenas noche, Bailey Cohen. Tempranito mañana."

"Por favor. Yo voy a ser la que te despierta."

And, indeed, there she is, tapping my foot a las seis y cuarto de la madrugada with my head pounding like a ghetto blaster. As if the pounding isn't enough, it's not even eight in the morning, I haven't even clocked in yet and Schecter's on me, asking why I'm walking in with one of the tenants.

"You said yourself yesterday she wasn't a tenant."

"Don't get smart with me, Castillo. You know what I mean. No luce muy bien que--"

"¿Que que? That I offer someone who needs assistance assistance? Or better we let her spend another night with her abusive boyfriend because mami y papi can afford the rent here."

"Excuse me?"

Mi cago en la suerte. At the end of the day, I need this job, and don't have the luxury of speaking up too much. That's a one-way ticket to picking grapes out in the Redlands. The year-round air conditioning of Las Brisas lobby has spoiled me demasiado.

Schecter steps closer. He's so short, we're eye to chest.

"There are two of us inside this office right now. Remember who in here needs the job most."

El muy hijo de puta. Si pudiera, I'd have strangled him right there inside his office.

There are many things I've had to learn in this country. One of them is swallowing my pride. "I'm sorry, sir."

"Not enough, Castillo. I need you, on your word, to tell me it's not going to happen again."

"I swear, sir. It will not happen again."

Schecter doesn't even look at me when relaying the day's tasks, spitting out a string of commands, enough to make sure my day is filled start to finish.

Bailey lingers in the hallway, and I have to tell her through text message what's happened.

Tranquilo. Have a lot to do. Will be in contact. Figure it out later. Todo a su tiempo.

Estas gringas and their ability to just let life happen as it will. Que sabroso debe ser vivir asi. She gets to make a living doing squat thrusts with ricachones, and I have to stand around unclogging a kitchen sink, helping change the flat on Mrs. Farkas' Tesla, killing cucarachas cornered in a bathroom, recommending nearby Cuban restaurants, and helping Mrs. Farkas again. This time carrying several packages from her weekly, direct-from-Italy, shipment of top-quality skin creams. I bet their active ingredient is dead immigrant-baby fetuses. En lo que se gastan dinero estos gringos ricos.

I'm wiped by lunch time. I sneak out to the car and message Bailey she can spend the night again if she needs, but she's going to have to find a way to make it to my place. Rideshare service.

Within the minute, she texts back: *Thank you so much. This won't be for longer. Til I find un lugar nuevo. Te puedo pagar renta meantime.*

After break, I come back into the lobby through the service entrance so Schecter doesn't see me right away. Between his lecture this morning and la tomadera de anoche, I'm ready for bed. My body doesn't bounce back from notas like it used to.

Schecter's nowhere to be seen, and the lobby doesn't have much action going on. So, I sit at the couch all the way at the back, where Bailey was going to sleep the night before and make fists with my toes; in, out, in, out. A trick I learned from my favorite movie *Die Hard*. It actually works.

Halfway into the fifth foot fist, someone at the main entrance shouts, "Oh my God. Oh my God. He fell."

Someone else hollers and it seems the whole lobby runs out to the street.

It's not uncommon in Miami for broncas to break out de un momento a otro. Ni en Cuba yo vi eso. I'm too tired to make a big deal of it.

Pero la gente run out from the elevators now, pointing at

the building across the street. Que carajo esta pasando? The crowd spills onto the other side of Collins.

I'm halfway down the lobby when Bailey dashes past.

La sigo lo mejor que puedo as she pushes through the middle of the tumult.

"Dios lo ampare, está muerto! Tan joven y que manera de morir." A woman screams out from somewhere behind me.

Por fin, veo la razon that everyone's out here on the middle of busy Collins, in the middle of a Wednesday afternoon. El chamaquito is lifeless, staring up to heaven, both eyes open. One fully intact, the other bloody and jellied. Blood trickles from his ears. A woman screams. ¿La misma de antes? So many screams, there's no way to tell.

Bailey says, "Gabe?" There he is, on his phone, calling for help.

Y ahi, me viene la sensación. Black bars, like in DVD movies, come into view and box the picture in. Once those bars close, they open again with me en el piso como un saco de papas. I have to calm down and not pass out. There's not enough oxygen in the room. ¿Que cuarto, mongo? Estas afuera.

Emergency sirens pierce the air as people scream for cops, paramedics, the boy's parents. For someone, anyone, to do something as if it will help this chamaquito who is too dead for anyone to do anything for.

No se callan esta gente. Their voices merge into a cacophony of worry, hysteria, tears, and panic. Son muchas voces. Too many people huddled together, all gathered around el chamaquito muerto, pushing us farther back until we're far from el muerto, let alone Gabriel. ¿Donde carajo se metio?"

"All the way from up there." Someone points up to the sky.

I look up and The Landings is the edge of a cliff and I'm Wile E. Coyote.

We have to get out of here.

"Bailey. Mija," I barely rasp. The tips of my fingers snap with those little jolts of electricity como si mi cuerpo is sending a message to itself not to pass out. The bars close in. Antes que todo se me ponga negro, I slowly walk toward the curb. Most people clear a path. A couple of aggressive machos tell me to watch where the fuck I'm going. I finally sit and lean my head as far between my legs as it will go. "Me tengo que sentar."

A hand gently pats my back. Antes de mirar pa' arriba, se que es Bailey.

"Bernardo. Sandy ha muerto. Gabe saw him."

I put my hands over my ears. The chaos of voices, sirens, screams, commotion es demasiado.

"¿Te puedes parar?" Bailey asks.

"No." Talking to her me ayuda slow my breathing. "¿Quien se cayo?"

"Un chamaquito que conocía."

"¿Se tiro?" I ask, because why else would a kid that age fall from that height if he didn't feel his whole world was over, como muchos de esa edad se sienten, muchas veces, en su vida sumamente joven.

"No. He would never do that."

Her sobbing helps me focus. I have to get up and help her out. Respira profundo: uno dos, tres. Extending my trembling hand out to Bailey, I know in a few seconds, I'll be up right. Primero, subo la cabeza so I'm looking straight at the main entrance of Brisas Canarias. Look at Schecter como todo un comemierda with his hand over his head.

Segundo, bend the knees and get that culo sticking up. What must I look like to everyone else? Coño, I'm the last thing they're looking at. I slowly extend my spine and take another deep breath as I bring my gaze toward the sky.

"Bien, bien. Poco a poco," Bailey says. "Respira."

Que pena. A young woman helping an older man through his anxiety.

"Ahora," Bailey says. "Come all the way up. Despacio. I've got you."

I clutch her hand and make one smooth movement back up on my feet.

"Estas bien?" She pats my back again and holds me there a couple seconds.

For some reason, the gesture hurts my pride. Que ridiculo. I force a smile.

Bailey sonrie for a couple seconds, then runs to the hedges lining the building to puke.

Vomita como si se hubiese comido una yegua. "Sacame de aqui," she says before falling back. I catch her and bolt for the car.

In the condo garage, I turn on the car and blast the AC a todo lo que da. "Do you know I knew that kid? El que se cayó."

"Claro que lo se."

"How do you know?" she asks.

"Me lo acabas de decir, Bailey."

She grips the seatbelt y suspira. "This feels better than being out there, Bernardo. Muchísimas gracias."

No se lo que decir pero se que it's better to say nothing at all. I put the car in reverse cuando del lado de Bailey alguien le pega un puñalazo a la puerta.

"What the fuck?' Bailey screams.

Gabe smiles. "There a party in here I'm not invited to?" Then to me, "What's up, ref? You sticking it to my girlfriend?"

I press the accelerator and peel out of there esperando que a lo mejor le arranque el brazo al so maricon.

As if reading my thoughts, he gives us the finger to confirm que no, no le arranque el brazo.

Como humo, we're out of the garage en una cacofonía de gomas chillando, Bailey laughing como loca, y el so maricon de Gabriel holding his phone up at us, screaming something we have no time to listen out for.

Gabe Acevedo

I don't want to see that bitch. It's been a long time coming and here's the straw that broke the camel's back. Fine, my parents own the place. Sure, I couldn't afford to live in a place like this if it weren't for my folks. All this is true. Either way, she made a commitment to start pulling her weight soon as her shit was together. This was close to a year back and, guess what, a banging body and a seasoned liver get quickly boring as fuck when the place is dirty and we're eating take-out most nights. It's not like she's working eight hours a day. She has time to at least keep the place up. I'm not going to be anyone's sugar daddy. No way. No how. I may be an idiot, but I'm not a fucking idiot.

Her reaction when I give her an ultimatum? Off to someone else's house to get blattered and send me petty pics of the empties at the end of it. Like I'd be shocked she's drinking. So, Bailey Cohen is out of here. Hasta la vista, baby. Don't let the glass revolving doors hit your ass on the way out.

Guess what, putita? I can be petty too.

Can't catch a wink after our fight, so I check the hospital employee portal and see there's an open early shift. Perfect. I'll work some extra hours, earn extra cash I'll spend on myself, come home to an apartment I can finally enjoy by myself. Blast porn in the living room at full volume if I want.

I leave a note for Bailey on the door at the ass crack of dawn and take off.

Mount Sinai is *the* hospital on the beach, so the emergency room is always jammed, with barely a moment to piss. Lunch breaks you eat standing up with one ear cocked for code blues. Fifteen minute breaks? Ha! Fucking forget it. You want the rainbow, you gotta put up with the rain, right? This job keeps me from completely mooching off my folks.

Truth is, I'm totally mooching, and I guess it gives them the right to peek in like they do every once in a while. Although, the last couple of times, Mom just showed up without notice. That I didn't like, but what the hell am I to do? I'm living rent-free in a condo that's just over a mil. And that was back in the days before the boom down here.

Mom and dad are all right. They don't get self-righteous too often, but when they have lately, their go-to is Bailey's crashing here rent-free.

"We're feeding two birds with one stone," Mom likes to pipe up. Whatever the hell that's supposed to mean. She's her own biggest fan.

Bailey contributes, but, let's be honest, it's on one of those "when I can" situations, which gets spotty, and old, real quick. She's a good cook but forget that old adage. The way to a man's heart is not his stomach. Not this man's, anyway.

It's a good spot to be in, on the best strip of the beach. I don't want to leave and doing it solo means settling in North

Beach, between 70 and 80th streets: the asshole of Miami Beach. That's a good strip, if you're looking for a gram and a toothless-crackhead blowjob. Not for me, thank you very much.

Bailey's drinking's gotten to be a mission, too. It was cute when we first met. When the worst it'd do was get her so horny, she'd beg to pull over so we could have a quick one on the side of the road. Now, the booze sours her. Inviting friends over, quickly getting sloppy. By the end of the night, she's the only one partying, dancing, and slurring lyrics along to whatever concert she's streaming. Then she slips into bed and wants to fuck when I've got work in, like, four hours. FUCK that.

Chaos no longer gets me hard like when we met. Instead, I feel bad, worry about her judgement. My own for keeping her around this long. Truth is, the Bailey Cohen I met—who'd keep me out all hours of the night, make me want to get up in the morning and cook breakfast, see what wild things she'd planned for the day ahead— is now someone I prefer to avoid. Being locked up in my room to catch up on sleep is more fulfilling.

It's been a long time coming. That she can't deny. She's not going to change. How many times has she promised and it never sticks?

Now it's time for her to go. This time for real. I'm being real nice by not throwing all her shit out the door and having Sheldon see her pick up after herself.

The hospital is, weirdly, the slowest I've ever encountered. Most people coming in with the flu or what they think is the flu, but nothing like nights, where you see some of the crazy spillover that happens when tourists come down and swallow more of South Beach than they can digest. It might look real cute on whatever ghetto-ass reality show marathoning on VH1 but South Beach will quicksand you real quick if you ain't careful.

This shift was so calm at Mount Sinai, at one point I was able to sit and drink coffee the whole way through without interruption. It was so slow, Megan, the floor manager I've been wanting to bone since new-hire orientation, told me I could leave early. I mean, that's just unheard of.

"You sure?"

"Absolutely, there's like an hour to shift change anyway. Trust me."

Thrust her is more like it.

The possibilities ahead now with the whole place to myself and Bailey out of the way. Man, it's going to be fun, fun, fun.

Megan's ass cheeks clenching my face is what I'm thinking of as I wait to turn left onto Collins. Determined to whack it as soon as I get upstairs.

As I'm approaching the side street leading to the condo's resident parking, something slams into the concrete in front of the building across the street. I know that thing's a body before even turning my eyes on it. Nothing else falls like that. I park in an empty street spot and run across to The Landings.

Somehow, I'm the first one there. For a split second, it's just me and the body alone in the world. I'm closest to the body, with just enough of a gap between me and the others approaching. Someone screams, and this becomes the scene of a tragedy. This is my tree falling in the woods. As if time stopped and no one's around but me for a blink of an instance. Something tells me to pull my phone out, aim, and snap. And I do. Two pictures of the body.

"What the fuck was that?" someone shouts from behind me.

I put the phone to my ear—pretending my first intention was to dial 911 and not preserve the gruesome image for ever and ever—and call it in. Glass shards trickle down from the balcony rail that's twisted metal jutting high above.

I tell the middle-aged lady to step back, not come any closer as if I care her old ass walks into an anxiety attack. Then she shouts at the rest of the crowd running toward her to stop right where they are. Metal might come crashing down any moment.

As I explain to the emergency operator that a body just happened out of the sky, more people file out from every condo within the perimeter until a crowd's gathered, pushing me back. With so much hysteria, people clamoring, and no one actually doing anything, I snap a couple more pictures. If anyone sees, they don't say shit.

The operator tells me the switchboard is lighting up with calls about the same incident. I hang up to her assuring me emergency crews are on their way. Sirens pierce the distant air.

The growing crowd seems to swallow the body as it pushes me back. It's Bailey's friend. That dumb kid always fucking around like Bruce Lee. How high is that? I cock my head up way too fast and am immediately dizzy. Jesus Christ did that fucking kid plummet.

As I park back in the garage, Bailey's not answering her phone. The fuck is she? Soon as I get upstairs, I run out to the balcony to get a bird's eye of the cluster fuck.

It's a cacophony of noise and movement. Emergency sirens, people crying, even a couple running off to the bushes at the side of the building to puke. I'm getting it all on camera, zooming in as much as I can and panning over to the vomiting couple.

It's Bailey and the maintenance guy. Can't remember his name and it doesn't matter, but I do know they've been getting tighter and tighter with each fight we have. Now, she's consoling the pussy while he retches into the bushes. Got her. That's where she must've spent last night, rubbing it in my face with her stupid ass messages in the middle of the night. Welp, she'll get hers. I pan back to ground zero where police have started cordoning off the area, doing their best to move people back and keep the body covered. They have a time of it with so many people clamoring to get a shot of Collins' fallen Icarus.

I press stop record as the ambulance doors close and its siren pierces the air. The tumult of people parts in an organized, surprisingly considerate, way. Why turn on a siren for a dead body? It's most likely headed to a cold slab in the Mount Sinai mortuary.

Bailey and Bernardo cross the street back toward me. Opening the tracker app I installed in her phone when she started drinking to concern a few weeks ago, I see they're both headed to the garage. I bolt down there faster than I've ever run for anyone, because fuck her. And, wouldn't you know. There they are, sitting in his car together, so comfortable in one another's company. I wait behind a column and watch, waiting for the right moment to… Bailey grabs that undocumented prick's hand.

They jump up, caught, when I slam my fist against the window hard. My intention is to smash it into spider web glass. It crushes my hand instead, but I'm too pissed to feel anything except the rage boiling up in me, ready to pop like that dead kid's head.

Praying to God this beaner gets out of the car to start some shit, so I can beat his ass and have him fired. Schecter and my parents know each other real well. One phone call and this maintenance man is out on his ass, Bailey Cohen along with him.

Bailey yells some shit I can't hear. She's always being extra. Janitor's eyes go wide as he lurches that bitch into reverse and peels out like The Italian Job. I'm surprised he's literate enough to read the gear shift letters.

Reminding them who's boss, I take the phone out my pocket and pull up one of the pictures of the dead boy. "Look who lost her fucking friend. Splat!" I yell. They're too hysterically busy trying to get away from me to hear. She'll know soon enough.

In the elevator, I start crying, hoping no one walks in. My impulse to destroy folds over into tears. Let Bailey and Emiliano Zapata do whatever they want to one another.

I sit in the living room and cry like a bitch. I mean sobbing so hard, it takes me a few minutes to register the disgusting scent. Weed and curry. Two things that perfectly sum up that bitch Bailey Cohen. Two smells in this world I've come to hate so much because they instantly transport me back to her beautiful body, her annoying penchant for exercise, the way she can strike up a conversation anywhere we go, while I'm left nursing a tepid beer in the corner. I give her damn near a year of my life inside this apartment rent-free and this is how she goes out? Hotboxing me inside my own house? She's got another thing coming. Thank you, Bailey Cohen, for freeze drying these tear ducts, bitch.

I dial Elias, the stoner kid who works with me, always looking for extra shifts for extra cash. He follows around some hippie band every summer and lives the in-between months working and saving for the three-month rage. From the stories I've heard in the breakroom, kid gets pussy up the wazoo during those runs. Rumor has it the kid also has a side gig knocking off scrips he sells off duty. Like a regular cockroach; anything to make it.

"Yo, what's up, Gabe? Calling out? Need me to cover for you?"

"No, but I got a way we can both make money."

"All ears, broseph."

He says annoying shit like that all the time. "You're about

to get a dead kid coming in."

"The fall? Yeah, he's here already."

"Perfect. That's Ximena Mangual's kid."

Nothing.

"The telenovela actress."

"Dude, I don't really watch much TV."

"Doesn't matter, man. Point is, we can make a lot of money if we get some pictures. I already got pictures of the body. Can you get some more? Maybe pictures of the parents?"

"How much?" Stoner asks.

"Fifty-fifty split on whatever we make."

"I'll see what I can do. Fifty-fifty the whole way?"

"Right down the middle."

"Give me til end of shift."

Perfect. Now to get Bailey Cohen out of my life forever. I walk to the kitchen and grab one of her favorite bottles of wine, uncork, and swig straight from the bottle. She's left all her shit neatly organized by the door. The kid must've come crashing to earth as she was packing. I open the balcony doors and living room windows wide as they'll go, get the disgusting funk out. An hour wanes as I work through a first, then a second bottle. For the second hour, slowly tearing at her clothes, picking apart her knickknacks. I especially take my time with her fitness shit. Anything that has to do with her livelihood, I slowly rip them apart, thinking of every difficult moment, every second of drama she brought into my life and continues to now. As I'm about to uncork a third bottle, contemplating burning her shit right outside the balcony, Elias calls back.

"Dude, it's done." he says, voice quaking like he just finished running a mile.

"Did you get what I asked?"

"Yeah, man. Two of the kid lying dead by himself and a couple of the grieving parents."

"That's it?"

"What do you mean that's it? If you want more, dude, you're going to have to get those yourself."

"Don't get lippy with me, motherfucker."

"I need you to commit right now and promise we're splitting this bitch fifty-fifty."

"What's wrong with you?" Gabe asks.

"This is weird, man."

"You work at the emergency room of a hospital," I remind him. "Don't start acting like a bitch now."

"Fifty-fifty, man. I need to hear you say it."

"Fuck, man. Yes. Fifty-fifty. Soon as you send them, 'cos right now I got no reason to believe you."

"Call me soon as you get a bid."

"Send them."

"Right now," he says. The confidence in his voice has waned with each line so now it's almost a whisper.

My phone dings.

"Sent. So I'll hear from you firs—"

I hang up on the asshole. I hate having to repeat myself over and over again just to reassure someone.

The first two pictures are of the kid. Looking much more peaceful than when I saw him fall. I mean, how they cleaned him up, you'd never know he rocketed over ten stories. Think the cliche you hear about corpses looking like they'll wake up any moment. . . That. Looks like he's sleeping. You can tell the left side of his face popped like a grape on impact. Knowing what they had to start with, it's a masterpiece. The other two pictures are the parents in mourning. One, they stand over the body. The other, the famous grieving mother wipes tears under darkened sunglasses. Got to give it to Elias, the kid can sneak pictures like no one's business. Takes fucking nerve to do what he did. Fucking cockroach. No wonder he was having a one-to-one with his guilty conscience. I'll make sure he feels it's worth it.

With this kind of result, fuck it, time to uncork that third bottle into hour numero tres, as Bailey and that dick would say. Dick's probably uncut. Raising a toast to myself. Here's to life post-Bailey. Here's to freedom. I drink out on that balcony, until the masses huddled below blur into trails and my stomach starts turning in on itself. My judgment so rotted, I drink a little more to help it pass, because, why not? How the hell do people like Bailey make a lifestyle drinking so much? I drink until I end up on the bathroom floor, on my knees, hugging the toilet seat. Retching out so much purple vomit, I wipe my nose of cabernet-colored snot. The room's spinning. I'm able to make it to bed, close my eyes, and count myself to sleep.

And wake up the next morning, taking my sweet time. Before doing anything at all, I call the hospital staff line and amp up the grogginess in my voice to let them know I won't be coming in. The operator says no problem, she's got coverage, hopes I feel better.

Outside on the balcony are the three empty bottles from the night before. I have a right mind to chuck them to the street below, onto the huddled mass still gathered at the makeshift memorial that quickly sprang up overnight. Kid had a lot of friends, or maybe just people hoping to get their pictures on local media, one step closer to fame, three degrees of separation.

Time to cash in myself. Over coffee, I scour the Internet for tabloids willing to pay the highest price for exclusive content.

Surprise, surprise, the highest bidder is out of Brazil. *O Respingo's* website practically begs i-journalists for good pop-culturally relevant images; promising: *MUITO DINHEIRO!*

Dialing out through a networking app that keeps my number anonymous, I'm on the horn with *O Respinga's* pop culture editor in no time. Pablo Porras spits out a couple of lines in Portuguese.

"Speak English," I say.

"What's up?" he says.

"I have pictures you'll be interested in," I say.

"Lots of people say that every day. Of what, bro?"

"The kid who fell out of the high rise."

"Miami?"

"Yes," I proudly say.

"Ximena Mangual's kid?"

"Very one."

"What we talking about here?"

"The body, on the floor, right after it fell. Up close and personal. Muito sangue. Pictures in the hospital, of the body. Pictures of his famous mother looking muito triste."

"No way. Send them over. I need to see these pictures are what you say."

"One picture, Pablo. For your eyes only. Show it to anyone else before we make a deal and I swear I'm coming over on the next flight to stick my foot straight up your Brazilian bundo."

"Relaxar, irmão. Send one picture right now. I'll look it over with you on the phone. If I'm interested, we talk business. If not, we do not."

A few seconds after I hit send, Porras whispers, "Puta merde. You weren't kidding. How'd you manage?"

"Don't worry about that. You want the rest?"

"Are they like this?"

"Exclusive, mi irmão."

"How does five hundred each sound?"

I send my digital account information and am almost a month's-worth of work richer in minutes.

I call Elias and lie about his final cut.

"Fuck that. I haven't slept since I sent them. Let's just pretend it never happened. Please. You don't know me. That's my payment," he says.

What a punk. Even better.

"Sure thing. I'll see you when I see you."

The street between my building and the scene of the tragedy is cordoned off. So many people down there. A beehive of the kid's friends, maybe. More likely, judging from what I can see up here, it's people descending on the place to be seen on any camera belonging to any journalist anywhere in the world.

No time like the present to cash in on fifteen-minute whores. Chugging the rest of the coffee that's gone tepid, I raid one of the junk boxes shoved into the back corner of my walk-in closet. Flipping that bitch is digging through an archive of past hobbies. I'm nothing if not compulsively impulsive. Buried underneath shake weights, golf discs, and a couple of freshwater aquarium starter manuals, I find the digital camera mom and dad gifted me many Christmases back, when that amateur photography course consumed me. There's an SD card inside with old pictures of a Halloween party with a girl from exes past. No image worth keeping, so I delete it all and head downstairs, into the guts of this makeshift memorial.

Surprise, surprise. It's mostly teens inside the nucleus. School mates and friends of the poor victim. Most on the outer bands are fans of his famous mother, who I wouldn't know from Eve.

A young girl with pink hair asks me to snap a picture, asking me to please be sure and get the beam of sunlight cracking through Collins' highrises. I tell her if she wants to be beautifully lit, she needs to be born again. Her partner, whose sex I can't decipher, steps in front, between me and pink hair. "Say, man," he/she says, "There a problem here?"

I step close, balling the fist not holding the camera. "You tell me, Ellen Degeneres. Do we?"

Their eyes go wide as pink hair pulls them away. "Leave that asshole alone. Some people just want to start shit wherever they go."

I smile wide and keep my eyes trained on them as they disappear into the mass of similar uncertain identities. Working my way around, rather than through, and throwing the occasional elbow, I'm able to get close to the makeshift memorial at the sight of the fall, where I first saw the kid on the ground, splattered open.

NEVER FORGET NUESTRO HERMANO, SANDY MANGUAL.

It's written out in sidewalk chalk, each letter a different pastel color. The text is bordered with pictures of Sandy posing fake gangster, hugging up on female friends, planting a wet one on mom's cheek.

I snap away as much as I can before I'm pulled back by the collective mass.

Some of the older folks wave at me. I don't return the favor. Because, fuck 'em.

Pablo Porras chimes out an eager, "Gaaaabriel, my

clandestine journalist in Miami. We posted the pics. Seen them yet?"

"No."

"Check 'em out, dude. They're getting us the most traffic since nine-eleven, bro. Buzz from all over the world."

"Good because I have more."

"Perfect. What are we talking about?"

"Downstairs at the memorial. People of all ages crying, holding one another. Lot of his mom's fans. Pictures right at the spot he fell. You can still see a little blood."

"Naaah. Sorry, bro. I can just turn the TV on to see that. We need what no one else can get. Exclusives, man. Nitty-gritty. Blood and guts. That first stuff you sent me was gold. Weegee type-shit."

"But. . ."

"I have to go, irmão. Busy news day. Hit me up again when you have stuff like what you sent this morning." He hangs up.

Weegee?

Arthur Fellig, known by his pseudonym Weegee, was a photographer and photojournalist, known for his stark black and white street photography in New York City.

That's according to Wikipedia. A click on the images search tab gives me the answer to what Porras wants. What did I expect from Brazilians? All you get over in South America is a bunch of savages thirsting for blood. Look at Bernardo Castillo. That's the only reason that dude is with Bailey, probably looking to stick his big immigrant pene inside a fresh, (not so much), innocent, gringa.

O, Respingo's got my images front and center. Pride blankets me as I look at Sandy's pictures. So good on first click, they haven't been cleaned up at all. Not one edit or digital manipulation. Pure unadulterated me, nit and grit, no filter.

I think about the cesspool that is Miami. How much I hate it after thirty years. Even from prime real estate like mine, it's a disgusting, trashy city with savagery right outside the doorstep. Just point and click. A city like this takes a lot out of someone; trust, innocence, sanity, hope, ambition. It's time to take some of that back. Pretend I'm on safari. Venture outside and let the animals take care of the rest. I'm just the anthropologist capturing it all. Be the first on scene, don't get in the way, snap some good pics, and get paid hand over fist by every other Pablo Porras out there. In time, I can leave the hospital, work for myself, and spend my days up here, with no one to bother me, no one to tell me what to do for the next eight hours. Just me and myself.

I send Bailey a link just to be sure she sees the images I was trying to show as she sped off with her new boy toy.

Within minutes, she's calling and, for curiosity's sake, I let that bitch ring because, if nothing else, I know her so well. As predicted, she keeps calling. Can't keep away from a fight. After the fifth call, I pick up.

Because, fuck her.

Las cosas se calmaron

Once out of the garage, I constantly check my rearview because un gringo como Gabe is crazy enough to follow me all the way home and the last thing I need is someone like that knowing where I live. Estos Americanos son mas locos que el carajo.

"No es gringo," Bailey corrects me. "His parents are Colombian."

"Even worse."

"But they don't show any ties at all to the country. He's never been there, doesn't speak Spanish, has no idea what a bandeja paisa is."

It doesn't make me feel better. Not until la madrugada when everything is quiet as Bailey tries to get a hold of el fallecido's parents. Ninguno de los dos hablamos a word about it since getting to the house. What's to say? We both saw what we saw and in instances like that lo mejor es quedarse calladito. So, we sit on the couch finishing the beers left in the fridge. De vez en cuando, she cries. She leans in once and I hold her. Otherwise, la dejaba tranquilita. When the beers are through, she quietly asks if there's a liquor store nearby.

Pointing her in the direction of El Gato Tuerto, I ask if

she needs a ride and don't push when she says she'd rather walk by herself.

El Gato Tuerto is right around the corner, so I stay outside, echando un vistazo as she walks down. The neighborhood isn't terrible pero uno nunca sabe en este Miami. Mucha gente here like to talk about Cuba like they know what's going on on the island, but I've never felt as unsafe back home as here. So many people like to own guns like they're preparing for una revolucion. Por eso, I keep an eye on her.

She walks as if something is pulling her shoulders down to earth. Como si tuviera lead weights in her shoes and yo without a goddam clue what to say. If I can't get the image of that chamaquito dead on the floor out of my head, and I didn't even know him, que carajo is she feeling? Bailey walks back the same way she'd gone, con la mirada para el piso.

We drink until the next day. No tv, no radio, just conversation. Hablando tremenda mierda.

I'm not the type who can drink and drink without eating. By lunchtime, tengo un hambre perra. "¿Quieres algo de comer?"

"Sopa de pollo."

"Sopa de pollo grande. Got it."

"Pequena."

Pequena isn't enough para la muela derecha, but I'm not going to push it. In a few days, I'll try snapping her out of it.

Ni modo. She snaps out of it before the last sip of her sopa, gasping so loud at her phone, pense que she was choking on a bone. "That fucking asshole."

"¿Que pasa?"

"¿Que pasa, Bernardo? Que Gabe Acevedo es un maricon de mierda. A man with no kind of ethics whatsoever."

Me vira el teléfono y tengo que acercarme to see. Lo primero que veo is the headline:

Tragédia em South Beach!

Lo que veo is something que mas nunca se me borra de la mente. The same image of the kid from the day before, tirado en el piso, splayed out for everyone to see in his last moments, ensangrentado, cagado, un ojo hecho mermelada. I don't read Portuguese but it's close enough to Spanish for me to know the first line introduces the victim as the son of Ximena Mangual. Antes que pueda leer mas, Bailey pulls the phone away and is dialing out to el so maricon de Gabriel, who, of course, does not answer.

Sigue llama que te llama until on the third one, I reach for the phone. "Bailey, porque mejor…"

"¡No me toques, Bernardo, o te lo juro!" She pulls the phone back in a fist and I think she might hit me, so I step back. Hay un momento de pausa antes que se desinfla. "I'm going to get a hold of this motherfucker."

A la quinta llamada, el muy descarado le contesta. She doesn't give the guy a chance to say one word. He lit the fuel que se había estancado overnight.

After she hangs up, she walks to the fridge, pounds a beer, and says, "Dame las llaves."

"Estas loca, Bailey." It is not a question.

"Maybe, but both of you are fucking crazy if you think I'm not going to do something about this."

She starts for the door.

"Where are you going?"

"To pay Gabe a visit."

"No."

"Fine." She walks out in the direction of the beach.

Un aviso sobre Bailey Cohen. La mujer tiene tremendo timbales. I mean, she would make a lot of guys I know recoil in intimidation, este mismo incluido. She says she's walking to the beach, there's no reason to think she's doing it for attention. The girl is actually going out to the beach on foot. What am I going to do? Let her go out there sola? And do God knows what to this crazy gringo of an ex-boyfriend? Takes a guy just as crazy to date someone like Bailey Cohen for that long, so no me queda otra que seguirla y convencerla to get in the car.

"What are you going to do?" I ask on the way. Instead of the highway, I take bottom streets, buy me some time a ver se la puede convencer a calmarse.

Instead, it works the other way. "¿Porque carajo te montaste por abajo? These fucking people, this God damn traffic, is only pissing me off more."

"Calm down, mija. Por favor. You're—"

"I'm not your mija. Don't tell me what to do and don't tell me what I am." She turns and glares at the side of my face.

Even though I'm on a red and can look at her, I refuse. No tengo los timbales.

"Y cuando lleguemos, no te atreves a cruzarte conmigo. ¿Me entiendes? I came to do what I came to do. And I'm going to do it."

I nod at the streetlights whizzing past.

"I need to hear you say it, man," she says.

"I will not get in your way, Bailey Cohen."

"Promise me, Bernardo Castillo."

"Te lo prometo, Bailey Cohen."

Le suena el teléfono. She just listens hasta que el tipo le cuelga.

"This fucking asshole," she whispers. "He destroyed all

my shit."

"Bueno, you did smoke his place out y empaparlo en curry."
She giggles.

"No te mereces nada de esto," I tell her.

I park in my spot in the garage. Damn near nine o'clock. There's something about this building after nine que me eriza. I can't explain it, it gets super quiet, and the lobby seems like no one lives there.

"Esperame aqui," she says.

"No jodas. You can do what you want, but you're not going to stop me from going with you."

"This could get you into serious trouble, Bernardo."

"You're the one who can't get into serious trouble. ¿Me entiendes?"

She smiles, as much as she can given the situation. "Do not interfere, Bernardo. Promise me you're—"

"Bailey Cohen, te lo juro. May I lose my job tomorrow if I interfere in whatever you're going to do."

"If I can strangle him?"

"Te cuento los segundos, just to be sure it's done."

"Andale."

La muy espabilada se sabe el camino para que Schecter no se de cuenta, a service elevator for the cleaning staff to use so residents won't be bothered by their comings and goings. Half the size of the residents' elevator. Right up to the twenty-third floor. The closer we get, the more intranquila se pone. Stepping up on to the balls of her feet like she's in the middle of a set; uno, dos, tres. Breathing in through her nose and out her mouth. Mientras tanto, yo como estúpido, sudando debajo el pull over, armpits growing damper, sweat dripping to my lower back.

¿En donde terminara esto? Suena el timbre. Vigésimo tercer piso. Camino detrás de Bailey y hacia al apartamento del so maricon, sabiendo muy bien que cuando todo esto se despliegue, después del arroz con mango por venir, ninguno de nosotros terminaremos iguales. Cada uno cambiado, cicatrizado.

¿Hasta donde llega la rabia de una mujer despreciada? Mas que eso; encojonada.

One, two, three. The knock on the door knocks me out of the daydream. Here we are. Whatever Bailey came to do, she's doing. It's happening. Footsteps approach the door, the lock and doorknob turn, the door pulls open.

Bailey kicks it in.

No se si la puerta llegó a darle directamente al so maricon, but it definitely knocks him back. In my shock, I stay outside a few seconds until Bailey screams. Not from pain, but rage. Either way, it's a scream, and she's my friend.

Cuando abro la puerta, Bailey's on the floor y el muy maricon towers over her. I can't see if he's smiling or what because his back is to me, to the door, which I shut, and fucking tackle the guy, para despingarlo todo.

Bailey screams at me. "No!"

Aqui si que no hay frenazo. I'm doing what I'm supposed. You know how people say in moments of rage they black out and don't come to until it's all over? Ni papa. As I rush up to the guy, so fast there's nothing he can do to stop me, I think of everything to lose: el trabajo, anonimato, la seguridad, residencia en estos Estados Unidos. Todo se ira a la mierda, en cuanto. . .

I've got him by the neck, squeezing it like an overripe orange.

El muy maricon gags. I don't want to kill him but, definitivamente, if I'm this far in, lo voy a desconjonar todo. One good fist in the eye because I remember what el chamaquito looked like in those pictures. I bang his head against the wooden floor una, dos, y tres veces, so he can feel, even slightly, what it must feel like to hit concrete from thirteen stories up.

"Okay, Bernardo. Cuidate," Bailey says.

¿Cuidarme de que? It's done. There's no turning back. You don't tell Beethoven how to compose. ¿Yo? I'm a master of destruction. Destroying other people, like I'm physically doing now to el muy so maricon. Para que sepa muy bien lo que pasa cuando se pasa de rayo. Destroying other people, like I metaphorically did to Eugenia. Bueno, ese fue Dios. Burlandose de mi, porque me pasé de rayo.

I don't know what's going to happen to Bailey after this, pero se bien que tambien, en alguna forma, la estoy destruyendo. Asi que no me queda otra but to literally destroy this asshole.

Y que bien se siente, tan natural, punching Gabe in the middle of that condescending smile, watching teeth and blood spill all over the nice, natural wooden floor of his parents' luxury high rise.

"You fucking spic," he manages to get out between streams of blood and spit pouring from his entitled mouth.

Este si que se las trae, so I kick him under the chin como Pele en el '59.

And that shuts him up. Puts him out actually. He's not moving, doesn't say a word. Just his left arm twitches, como rabo de lagarto.

"Lo mataste," Bailey says. It is not a question.

"No way."

Gabe starts retching really loud, nothing's coming out of

him, except for a lot of noise that will get us in trouble very soon if we don't—

"Vamonos," Bailey says.

I say, "There are cameras everywhere."

"That's right, you fucking spic, and they're going to—" Gabe starts and Bailey kicks him in the chin too, like Maradona in the late eighties.

El tipo cae redondo, un saco de papas.

"What do we do?" she says.

"I'm staying until the cops come."

"Aqui mismo me quedo," she says.

Todo se a hecho humo. He pulverizado todas las relaciones en mi vida que han valido la pena. Here's Bailey Cohen dragged into my shit world, just like Eugenia back home.

Y porque me sale del culo, I hit that motherfucker with my heel, right on the temple.

———

By the end of the night, I'm in jail, which feels like home because almost everyone in there speaks Spanish.

Last I saw of Bailey, she's promising to get me out of there quick. "I've got connections, Bernardo Castillo. You'll see."

"¿Que hiciste?" my cellmate asks.

"Una bronca. ¿Tu?"

"Le agarre el culo a una jeva en la universidad. ¿Te acuerdas los días que podías agarrar un culo y nada pasaba?"

I smile politely and turn over on my cracker-thin cot like I might get some sleep for the night.

"¿Que pasa? ¿Eres maricon?"

"Lights out," a guard yells.

I close my eyes thinking about how things were better off back home. Y, claro, back home daría cualquier cosa por venir aca.

From the top bunk, my cell mate keeps repeating, "¿Eres maricon?" Like some sort of mantra. Then starts jerking off and panting so obviously and furiously, I shut my eyes even tighter, praying for one of the orishas to take me far, far away.

Clang, clang, clang. A different guard taps on the bars and my cell mate is suddenly, almost-absently, quiet. "Castillo, you're going home," the guard says.

"What?"

"Te vas, mi hermano. Someone bailed you."

I don't move, trying to figure it out.

"Vamos, compadre, before I change my mind and leave you in there with Pablo Paja."

I'm up and out in no time to the diminishing sounds of my bunk mate prayerfully moaning, "¿Eres maricon?"

———————

Bailey looks completamente diferente from the last time I saw her. As I was being led away in handcuffs, parecía que iba a quemar el edificio entero. Now, it's obvious she's been crying since. Not softly to herself, either, but crying with a force to drown herself y decir adios ha todos los problemas que la rodean.

She orders an Uber and is quiet for the first ten minutes of the ride.

Cuando no puedo mas, pregunto, "How did you?"

"Not me. I put up half, someone else fronted the rest."

"¿Quien?"

"The Manguals."

"¿Como?"

"That's where we're headed now."

"Bailey, yo ni conozco a esta gente."

"Estan encojonados, Bernardo. I showed them the pictures and told them it was Gabe who took them. Le quieren partir la cara. They want you to help out."

"Pa' la pinga. Me llevas para la casa and I'm going right to sleep. Lo único que necesito—"

"This on your conscience?"

She holds the phone right in my face. Sandy Mangual's battered image stares back at me. I flinch.

"Yo no tome las fotos."

"No, pero el muy maricon de Gabriel lo hizo and he also did this to you," she points all around me like I'm a sad person to look at, as if I'm the offense.

She pulls the collar of her shirt so far down que por el momento pienso que me va enseñar mas de la cuenta. "And this to me." Where he had pulled on her before I got inside and kicked his ass, tenia tremendo morado. "Estuviste bien en partirle la cara. Los Manguales quieren seguir la vuelta."

"No entiendo, Bailey. Why me?"

"Te conocen bien, Bernardo. They like that you stood up for me, and that you stayed until the cops showed up. Hiciste mucho mas en esos quince minutos than Gabe has ever done in his life."

Muy bien, but what the hell are they going to ask of me? Who were these people besides famous names I'd heard on TV? ¿Que tanto saben de mi que me sacaron de la carcel y ahora quieren negociar como si yo fuera Clint Eastwood?

"This isn't right. I don't want to be part of anything else like tonight."

"Te van a pagar tremendas cañas, Bernardo. A los dos."

How many times had I heard so many promesas baratas? Only to have them pulled away as soon as the favor was complete. A mi nadie me va a tomar de comemierda mas en la vida entera. I suck my teeth.

"Si no me crees, por lo menos denles el chance. Te sacaron de la carcel."

"Pagaron la mitad."

"Por si tu decias que no."

She's right, I have to at least give them the benefit of the doubt. Oirlos bien, muy respetuosamente, antes de shaking my head and telling them very politely to fuck off. They just lost a kid. They're not thinking straight. Neither's Bailey. She's too angry, too close to the whole thing to see it for what it is: fucking stupid.

Por supuesto que quiero que Gabe termine en una carcel, agarrándose los tobillos a la petición de su cellmate pingu que se la mete sin vaselina todas las noches. Pero tampoco me chupo el dedo. Yo no vine ha este país a ser Clint Eastwood, ni Batman, ni ningún desgraciado Conde de Monte Cristo. Pa' la pinga con eso. Pero, Bailey's right in one thing. I at least owed it to them to listen while they pitched. They'd paid bail, after all.

Ximena Mangual's exactly what I expect, hiding behind dark shades like Jackie O despues que le volaron los sesos a Jack Kennedy. She smiles at me with a wave pero se queda al otro lado del cuarto, sollozando muy calladamente, like she doesn't want to bother anyone with her whimpering.

Bailey crosses the room without saying hi to the other two in there y le da un abrazo fuertisimo a la. . . ¿Viuda? ¿Como se le dice a un padre que pierde a un hijo? The thought goes away when Ximena starts crying mas fuerte todavia.

Looking away to give the ladies the privacy they might need, I look at the man in the kitchen, sitting on the wrap-around counter, un trago en mano. A este si lo conozco. En Cuba, hice plenty of research of all the things possible y este hombre is more important to me than Bill Gates and just under Warren Buffet en respecto a hombres que mas admiro. El Donald Trump portorro is what the Hispanic media like to call him. Of course, that's an insult now to every single accomplishment the man has made for himself and la raza. Si, yo se que muy rara vez se oye a un Cubano hablar tan orgullosamente. Pero, coño, this is Tomas Mangual we're talking about. El mismo who's designed and manages seventy percent of the San Juan skyline as we speak. El hombre tiene que tener por lo menos miles de. . .

"Bernardo! ¿Que te pasa, socio? Te estan hablando," Bailey says.

Ximena smiles underneath those big-ass cocaine sunglasses. "Mucho gusto, Bernardo Castillo. Yo soy. . ."

"Ximena Mangual" le digo, then turn to her husband, who's more important to me than all those people we passed on the way in, here's the guy los periodistas should be waiting to get a glimpse of. Not his wife. Aunque, sinceramente, nunca he visto ni un segundo de su trabajo. "Tu eres Tomas Mangual. Te conozco muy bien, señor."

He holds up his drink. De esa distancia, me parece ser whiskey. "Mucho gusto, Bernardo Castillo. Nosotros tambien te conocemos."

"El hombre que descojono a Gabriel Acevedo," Ximena says, then turns to Bailey. "What did you two decide on?"

"I haven't been able to explain it all to him yet."

"A ver, Bernardo Castillo. ¿Que precisamente sabes de mi?" Tomas asks.

"Eres tremendo para los negocios."

"Exactamente. Y ahora tenemos un negocio para ti. Sientate y toma conmigo."

Solo en estos Estados Unidos me encontraría brindando con el hombre que era mi faro when I dreamed of leaving the island and settling right where I am now. In America, yet farthest from the American dream than ever.

Tomas swigs the rest of his drink, pours another, y empieza con la muela. Only there is no bullshit there. He's talking but what he's saying isn't just talk, it's action. Through tears, gasps, and fleeting smiles at the mention of la tremenda chispa que tenia su hijo, nos dice que he wants me to do exactly what I did to Gabe Acevedo, but permanently put him out of any fledging journalism career he might be thinking of pursuing.

Después del tercer trago, nos dice que si, oímos bien. Gabe Acevedo se recordará del dia que si cruzo con los Manguales, promising me and Bailey a future better than any either of us could possibly imagine—let alone access—at that very moment. All we have to do is repeat exactly lo que paso en Las Brisas. Solo con mas relajo.

I finish my first drink. "¿Porque a mi, Señor Acevedo?"

"¿Sabes como llegue a donde estoy, Bernardo?" Tomas pours us another.

"Inteligencia."

"Curiosidad. I did some research, Bernardo Castillo. And I know who you were before you came here."

"What did you tell them about me?" Le pregunto a Bailey.

"We barely know you. We just know what you did. Which works perfect for what we're going to do," Tomas replies with a smile before swallowing his fourth drink down hard. The gulp resonates in the quiet room. "Well, one of us knows you better than everyone else here."

"Señor Castillo. Gusto en vernos de nuevo."

Reconozco la voz antes de virarme. No matter how much I run, which farthest corner of this earth I might tuck in, I will always, instantly, recognize that fucking accent. Janaina Brilhante.

Tomas pours a fifth drink.

I tap my glass on the counter to keep from ahorcando a la muy desgraciada de. . .

"Janaina tells us you two go way back."

My drink is done as soon as it's poured y le pido otro al Señor Mangual.

"Claro que si. She killed the love of my life."

No la puedo mirar, or any of them.

Camino hacia el balcon to finish the rest of what won't be my last drink of the night based on todos los fantasmas que me rodean. Outside, high above the world, shards still litter the tiled balcony floor. The railing that gave under Sandy's weight points to the pavement below like an accusatory finger. Beyond that horrific reminder, a wide-open, stunning view of the downtown skyline and Biscayne Bay. American Airlines Arena in the hazy distance, where the dreams of so many basketball fans have been filled and the pleas of so many homeless beggars ignored.

Tomas Mangual camina hacia mi. I see his reflection in the glass holding a fresh drink. Tomando con proposito. "Fucking maintenance de mierda promised they'd clean this by now. Can't trust anyone for shit these days. It's like they're rubbing it in our face." Empieza a llorar a moco tendido.

Ximena le sigue el paso, falling in a heap to the floor.

Bailey falls to her aid.

Janaina stands watching it all, blessed with a perpetual sense of narrative distance. . .

Muito desapego.

I don't have that luxury. No emotional distance here. Esa noche, I fall asleep to Eugenia's voice gritando. "Resingao, para de comer mierda y ponte las pilas. ¿A donde carajo se fue mi Cuca?"

En esos dias. . .

Tocabas la puerta dos veces. Yo respondía con tres golpes. Then, go around back and wait for me. Dimelo. ¿Que necesitas? Que lo tengo todo, hermano. Cigarros Americanos, europeos, chinos, cochinchinos. If it's rolled up to smoke, I got it. Playboys? Dale. Tirate tremenda paja. ¿Manteca 'pa concinar? Buen provecho.

Ahora. Eso si. No vuelvas por lo menos una semana. You get caught, we never met. I get caught, you're done. Mas te vale because I know people. How do you think I got all that shit? Want to stay in business for life? Keep people happy, give them what they need, and don't fuck them over doing it. That's the key. Whether you're tremendo yanqui en la yuma, Brasilero socialista, o te encuentras en completamente-al-reves Cuba. Don't fuck anyone over.

En esos días, me llamaban Cuca; corto para Cucaracha. Tenia tremendas ganas de salir de Cuba. hasta los cojones ya con la política, the struggle, snitches on every corner. Ya, pa' la pinga, Send me, us, somewhere else. Had it just been me, I'd have been out of there long ago, but I had an anchor to the island: Eugenia Cartas.

Mientras yo me sacaba un ojo por salir, Eugenia would never leave. It's the only thing she knew, ever. Aunque ya su familia la estaba dejando atrás poco a poco. They weren't leaving, but dying off. Thanks to her grandmother, we got the house. But the system, being what it is, let her keep it, as long as she opened it up to strangers.

Y asi fue que conocimos al muy hijo de puta, Anibal Cruces. Chivato de la fiscalia local del PNR. The first in line for weekly food distribution. As he passed, people's conversations muted. Once he'd passed by, las viajas supersticiosa se persinaban. And now he was our God damn roommate. And me running black market out the yard.

That's when I aggressively started pouring honey in Eugenia's ears. Teníamos que salir de la isla como relampagos.

"Ai, mi cielo. ¿Como pretendes hacer eso? Con que dinero?"

"I'm making money, mima. Hay otro lugares que no son Cuba."

"No para gente común y corriente como nostros," she'd say.

My good buddy Pavel was the connection. His wife Liria lived in Miami and was working on papers to have him permanently relocated ninety miles north. She'd come every two weeks with stuff, and constantly sent packages. Between her and Pavel's few buddies at the airport on our payroll, el negocio era fijo. In Cuba, anything steady is a blessing.

Liria loved to read and always flew down with a stack of books and magazines she'd just finished. Between those and the constant updates I gave her about Pavel's pending emigration, Eugenia started opening up about to the idea of viviendo en los Estados Unidos.

But she loved to counter. Holding up the latest edition of *Hola!* "Estos son celebrities, personajes de mentira. La gente común y corriente como tu y yo tenemos que trabajar dia por dia. ¿Crees que voy a tener tiempo de leer?"

"Don't worry, baby. I'll figure out a way. No vamos a la yuma a rompernos el culo."

Cuba's a den of hustlers constantly nickeling and diming to get by. El exilio uses this to go on and on about su propia gente. Que somos unos vagos que no quieren trabajar. Preguntan que se puede esperar de un grupo que no sabe lo que es levantarse a trabajar ocho horas seguidas, cinco días semanal.

¿Sabes lo que digo a eso? Come and spend one week here. Not en el Hotel Nacional o La Floridita. Come here, wake up, stretch, then mueve el culo to figure out how the fuck you'll make it through the day. Extrapolate that by three hundred-sixty four more days and then we'll talk. A pesar de lo que diga Radio Mambi, no somos criminales, ni vagos, ni chulos. Somos sobrevivientes. Every day we wake up to survive. El exilio se levanta a tomarse su cafe en el Pinecrest Bakery mas cercano y criticar un sistema que abandonaron sin vacilación.

Algunos en la isla pick-pocket, or triple-charge a cab ride from the airport to Old Habana. Las jineteras sell a couple hours to do with their malnourished bodies as you please. Y los turistas se aprovechan de esa desesperación. The girls we know tell me first-worlders are into some freaky shit y pagan por las narices. Alemanes y Japoneses especialmente.

Yo no tengo inclinaciones criminales. Ni soy muy bonito. Soy calladito, observador, y sumamente paciente. Pero eso si, tengo inclinaciones clandestinas. Hence, the name. You won't even know I'm close til you snap on a light and I'm scrambling away. While you're still with your big foot up in the air wondering a donde coño me fui.

Cuca. La cucaracha. What started as an insult for being a skinny, scrawny, sometimes unbathed, kid became a calling card to anyone in the neighborhood who needed what they couldn't find for themselves. The game was getting things for la gente en las calles. I needed to eat, so of course I charged but I tried to give mi gente the best possible prices. Remember, Glengarry Glen Ross? You don't sell a guy one car in five years, you sell him three over fifteen. Asi mismo.

That's my hustle in a den of hustlers. Even in this kind of environment, it's important to keep a moral code. Una linea clara, rígida, sobre la que no se pasa. Pero in this environment, mas que menos, te cruzas de vez en cuando con un hijo de puta como Anibal Cruces, que no tiene ningún tipo de código.

That's not fair, he had a mother and a family. One that sucked the system's pecker from the moment that train in Santa Clara derailed and the rebels descended on la Habana.

I was a cockroach, this guy was a goddam weasel and lately he'd been sniffing around my operation more than was comfortable. Making off-hand comments like, "Para alguien que no sale de la casa, tienes muchos amigos." o, "No he visto a fulanito en un tiempo. ¿Todo bien?" Knowing full well fulanito was popped last week trying to sell insulation tubing on the street. The weasel was also looking at Eugenia more than he needed to y si no se cuidaba. . .

"Estas loco," Eugenia would say. "¿Quien va estar mirando este culo de rinoceronte?"

We'd know each other since grade school. That's how it is around here. Desde entonces, everyone knew he harbored a serious crush.

Anibal was always trying to prove he was not what everyone knew him for. Through his connection en la fiscalia, he was tipped off to a Brazilian news crew who wanted to shadow him a few days and document the Cuban struggle, from the perspective of its strugglers, la gente en la calle.

"You believe that shit?" Eugenia said. She called *O Respinga,* "Noticias para blancos."

Think Latin America's answer to *Vice.* Yellow journalism peddled to a young demographic, without concern for journalistic integrity, informational accuracy, or relevance. Reporteros tatuados chupando un vape mientras caminaban por la vivienda del jefe del cartel de Oaxaca. In truth, nothing of vital information, lacking intellectual aesthetic. Just splash and flash to impress twenty-somethings with visions in their heads of el marimbero, la puta, y el chulo. They pumped out these ninety-minute documentaries all over the Internet once a week highlighting the dregs of a new exotic corner of the world. Y ahora, le tocaba a Cubita.

So, aqui venian a colocarse con el chivato del neighborhood y grabar mas de lo mismo. What was he going to do? Ask us permission? This was his way of showing he could have his own thing, matter to someone else. He loved every second of it, thinking it impressed the neighbors, more importantly, Eugenia. And we had to sit by and swallow the scene, with my black-market operation running full-tilt boogie in the yard.

He paraded that film crew como el papa. Introduced us as his roommates. We his. Not the other way around. Because, fuck us.

Yo no soy de mirar mucho a mujeres con no son mias, pero coño si la reportera Brasilera no era una de las mujeres mas bonitas que había visto en mi vida. Piel color de almendra tostada, pelo largo, negro como el carbon, y lizo como el de una china. Tan largo que se le caia hasta encima de un culito de manzana. Si se meneaba, te empapaba. Sabia muy bien lo que tenia y como usarlo. She had Anibal wrapped around her long, bony finger within five minutes. Had Eugenia not been there, a lo mejor a mi tambien. The cameraman was the tallest motherfucker I'd ever seen. He belonged on a national basketball team or inside the pages of Guinness.

Anibal introduced Janaina—que nombre—to Eugenia first. Cuando me dio la mano it was so soft and somehow cold to the touch. Gio, el camarografo, had the handshake of un carnicero. He was tall and skinny like a fishing rod, with the hands of a bricklayer.

"Bueno, mi gente," Anibal said. "I'm going to show them around the neighborhood. We might be in and out."

No me gustó nada la idea, I told Eugenia as soon as they were out the door. Pero ella, Dios mio, quedo encantada. As if she were the focus of the documentary, seeing herself in those celebrity magazines she'd devoured over the years.

"Que linda y que amable," dijo, mientras camino a la cocina and started tidying up.

"¿Que haces?"

"Limpiando for when they get back."

"Eugenia, no te das cuenta who they're following around? Do you know how much shit he's going to fill them with between now and whenever they get back?"

Los periodistas de otro país, hablando mas de un idioma, apuntando camaras, con sonrisas de un millón de dolares, made her feel, in the few minutes she'd known them, like a Kardashian. And, for our sins, she fell for it. I know Brasileros believe en santeria. I wondered if they'd worked some on her.

Thanks to reading so much, Eugenia tended to have a very positive outlook on life. Thanks to my line of work and lack of reading, era tremendo cinico. So, llame a Pavel y le dije que vinieran inmediatamente. Never have important discussions over the phone. Las lineas en Cuba have a way of frequently crossing.

"No, hermano. Tienes que ver la oportunidad que tenemos en frente. While he's entertaining this crew, he's out of the house and out of our hair, for. . .” Pavel stood in our living room now and turned to Eugenia. “¿Cuanto tiempo?”

“Yo me imagino no mas de tres dias.”

“Perfecto. That gives us good time. I won’t be here much longer. Me voy para la Yuma.”

Me cago en la. . . Felicidades para Pavel, pero sin el. . .

“Yo se que van a ver vacas flacas, pero vamos a ser lo mas que podamos. Esta semana, cualquier dinero que hagamos se queda con ustedes.” He turned to Eugenia, “Y para ti, tengo una sorpresa.” From the small of his back, he pulled out a copy of *Twilight*. She had been dying to read that book desde quien sabe. Reuso ver la película hasta que leyera el texto completo.

Our split of profits was normally forty-five, thirty-five. Pavel brought in the goods, he got the bigger cut. The remaining twenty percent was for overhead and business costs. No eramos millonarios, pero tampoco comíamos cable. Pavel was willing to give us that last week’s takings, which was huge. With what I had stashed, it was enough to get us off the island.

“¿Que pinga vamos hacer, Eugenia?”

“Lo mismo de siempre. Sobrevivir.”

“On what? Love and hope. Eugenia, let’s get the hell out of here. Please. No nos queda mucho mas en la isla.”

“No hay nada esperándonos en la Yuma,” me dijo, before sitting out on the porch to read the adventures of teenage vampi-lobos en Washington. For me, it was business as usual; tal cual.

We hustled until the sundown splashed the island that pink-purple color. There were very few things I held close about Cuba. Esa era una. En donde el mundo me pusiera, I’d always remember that sunset. The most beautiful in the world.

As me and Pavel counted the day's taking, double the usual, oímos a Eugenia reírse desde el porche. Escondimos el dinero en una lata de Chock Full of Nuts y la enterramos bien en el hueco cerca de la escalera, como siempre.

"Me voy, hermano," dijo Pavel. "No puedo arriesgar que me cojan."

Era Eugenia and the journalists, chismeando sobre su dia con el chivaton.

Anibal, sweating con un puerco, les pidio pasar por la casa pa' refrescarse. Eugenia took advantage of his absence to get to know the Brazilians better.

"Pensamos que eras Anibal," dijo Janaina with a start.

"Por favor." I scoffed. "En una pesadilla, maybe."

Janaina's eyes widened as she smiled. "Tu amigo es un poco—"

"No es nuestro amigo," I snapped.

"Um pervertido," Gio said.

"Si," Janaina said. "He seems eager to impress me."

"He's eager to impress everyone. No se acostumbra recibir atención de mujeres bonitas del extranjero."

From the corner of my eye, I felt Eugenia give me a look. She smirked too.

El camarografo smiled slyly too as Janaina looked down at the floor, apenada.

Eugenia was the most perfect woman I'd ever met, but si tenia un defecto, uno nada mas, era celoso con cojones.

"He tries to impress her by insulting me," Giovanni quipped. "A few more days and I might just have to. . ."

"Don't. Not if you want to complete this project without

interruption," I said. "Es hijo de puta, but he'll keep the right people off your back so they don't become the wrong people. Sino, you'll pay shooting tax after shooting tax. Y vuelven a Rio flat broke."

"We're from Sao Paulo," Janaina said, looking at me now with the confidence of correction.

Eugenia giggled. "Perdonalo. Geografia no es su area de expertise."

I shushed them. Over the years, the island and my line of work had turned me into a bat. Anibal closed the door to his room despacito, trying to listen in.

"Si van a tener alguien enseñándoles los alrededores, es Anibal." I stomped loudly on the porch planks; un, dos, tres. "He knows this area like clockwork," Then raised my voice mas de lo necesario. "Se conoce todo esto mejor que un cartógrafo."

In seconds, his footsteps tracked through the living room and out to us. "Oye. Respiren poco al entrar. He dejado una peste del carajo. Disculpen."

Everyone stayed quiet. Gio stared as if to strangle him.

Halo el teléfono de su bolsillo. "Mi gente, I gotta go. Se me olvido que tengo una cuestion urgente que no puede esperar hasta mañana." He turned to Janaina. "Same time tomorrow?"

"Of course. We'll be here."

Anibal winked. "Gracias, bellísima. Nos vemos mañana." El tipo bajó las escaleras del porche como Fred Astaire y, al llegar al fin de la pasarela, he turned and blew a kiss at Janaina, y después a Eugenia. Now I stared as if to strangle him.

"¿A donde va con tanto apuro?" Janaina asked once he was out of our volume.

"To give la fiscalia a detailed report about everything you guys discussed," I said.

"Espero que no le hayas dado mucha información personal," Eugenia said.

"Nothing can't be found with a quick Google search," Janaina said.

"Good. Asi es como se juega," Eugenia said. "Don't trust that guy far as you can throw him."

"¿Y tu, Eugenia? Can I trust you?" Janaina le pregunto a Eugenia.

"That's not for me to say," Eugenia said.

"I don't know you well enough," Janaina said.

"That's fair."

"¿Porque no me dejas conocerte un poco mejor?"

Eugenia beamed.

"I have a lot of work to do today and. . ." I started.

"Tu tienes mucho trabajo que hacer, Cuca. I can stay here and entertain our friends. La pregunta clave es, how are our friends going to entertain us?" She winked at Janaina, who blushed. If I didn't know any better, I'd get jealous.

"Cerveza," Gio stood and looked at me. "Please tell me there is beer here."

"Oh, there's beer," I said. "¿Porque no le damos un momento a las damas?"

Fuimos a la Bodega de la Esquina. That was the name of the place owned by Benny el Chino from whom mi abuelo compraba six packs. Es esos entonces, there was a lot more beer to choose from on the island.

"What's best here?" Gio asked. "On us."

"Bucanero." Strong and good for the Cuban heat.

Gio asked Benny for a case.

Asi se hace.

Insistió en cargar el case entero el mismo. "Anibal es un pervertido."

I chuckled.

"Whenever Janaina was turned around, he'd look at her ass and raise his eyes at me. Like I haven't been working with her long enough to notice myself. Cuando pasaba una mujer por el lado, he'd bump my elbow and make eyes too. Signal me to look at her tits, ass, or both. That guy doesn't think about much else."

"Para nada. He's out of it."

"We're not getting anything good out of him. Janaina doesn't want to tell him because then we've got nothing."

"If you don't have a good guide, olvidate," le dije, as we rounded the corner to hear Janaina and Eugenia filling the front porch with their laughter.

"I think that's what this is about," he said. "Janaina seems to think Eugenia might be able to give us more. Also, he would not stop talking about how you took Eugenia from him. Is that true?"

"In school, I may have been more charming than him."

As far as las señoritas, Janaina tenia *Twilight* en la mano, advirtiéndole a Eugenia que tuviera tissues listo para cuando llegara al final.

"Lo estoy leyendo despacito porque no se cuando pueda conseguir el segundo," Eugenia said.

"Yo te los envio cuando llegue a Sao Paulo," Janaina said, then turned to me. "Not Rio de Janeiro." She reached into the case and pulled a beer.

"Estan calientes," Gio warned.

"Don't care. Put a bunch in the fridge. Este no dura mucho. Tengo tremenda sed."

"Dame," le dije, taking the case from him. "Eugenia,

ayudame un momentico por favor."

"Pero—" empezo.

"Dos segundos."

"No me gusta esto para nada," I blurted as soon as we were in the kitchen, alone.

Spend enough time with someone, you quickly get to know them. The nuances that say everything sin tener que abrir la boca. Cuando Eugenia trataba de controlar su temperamento, hacia un gesto de no mirarte directamente a los ojos, sino mas arribita, en la frente. Era espeluznante y tremendo poker move. Everyone she did it to was thrown off their game y ella lo sabia muy bien.

She did it to me now. "¿Porque no?"

Dios me ampare.

"Si vuelve Anibal y te ve en medio de book club con su crush, sabes muy bien lo que va a pasar."

"Who gives a fuck about ese maricon? We know he's over there, cantando como loro, anyway. ¿Y que les va a decir, anyway? Que estuvimos hablando sobre los habitos amorosos de Edward Cullen y Bella Swan."

"Gio me dijo que she's trying to get information from you."

"Lo se. Jani me acaba de decir lo mismo."

"Jani? Look at you. ¿Since when has anything, aparte de libros, had you so googly-eyed?"

"Since something other than Cuba showed up at our door." She pulled three beers from the case. "These are for us. Hazle el favor a todos, pon unas cuantas a congelar, and come outside. Que hace tiempo since we have any guests que no son Pavel o Liria."

"Eugenia, por favor no vayas a—"

"Bottle opener, please." She wasn't looking at my forehead anymore. Directamente a los ojos.

"Esta bien. Pero, please, solo una noche, Eugenia."

"Si, comandante," she said in fake salute, and headed outside with room temperature beers.

"Oh, antes que se me olvide," she turned, leaning against the arch of the kitchen threshold. "Para de mirarle tanto el culo a la Brasilera."

"No jodas."

"Desde de que apareció, estas mira que te mira. Stop making it so obvious." She walked off.

"Mentira," I said behind her.

She walked out, middle finger high in the air.

I put a few beers in the freezer, the rest in the fridge. Back out on the porch, the three were laughing a carcajadas.

I sat and squeezed Eugenia's knee. "A ver," I said to Janaina. "¿Que te viene diciendo Barbara Walters?"

Janaina laughed.

"¿Que?" I asked.

"Barbara Walters es que la hace las entrevistas, mongo," Eugenia said. "En este caso, ella seria Barbara Walters. And I've just been telling her how much you've been staring at her ass since she arrived."

Las dos se rieron y Gio looked down at the floor, slowly shaking his head.

"I. . .No. Mentira." Blood rushed to my face.

Janaina raised her bottle and we all clinked.

"Bienvenida a Cuba," Eugenia said in general, then to Janaina. "Tranquila, que no es pervertido. He just appreciates a fine woman when he sees one. ¿Porque crees que me tiene a su lado tanto tiempo?"

Los Cubanos hablan horas y horas. Los Brasileros,

comparable. Over the next couple hours, we covered everything. Mostly, the girls talked books and celebrity.

Then, after her third beer, cracking a fourth, Janaina sorto la pepa.

"Oye, these are great stories. Why don't you go on record? Dejanos contar estas historias que de verdad tienen merito." Janaina said. "Anibal so far is just giving us what he thinks we want to hear. Cosas que lo engrandecen. We're looking for a story on the island, not on him."

"This can get us in trouble," I said. Then, to Eugenia, "Serious trouble."

"Si, me lo dijiste and I heard you loud and clear," she said. Then a los periodistas. "Perdonenlo. He's a little paranoid. ¿Entienden?"

"Of course. We will not reveal any of your personal information. No one will know who you are, at all."

Eugenia said. "¿Como pueden hacer que valga la pena?"

"Cash. Right now. More when it's over."

Gio pulled the wad from his camera bag. Between that and Pavel's earnings, era mas dinero que cualquiera de los dos habiamos visto en la vida. Enough to get to la Yuma and start over.

"Bernardo, a la cocina por favor," Eugenia said.

"Eugenia, mira. Yo se que estas teniendo. . ."

"Let's get out of here, Bernardo. There's nothing anymore. Janaina me comento que Anibal esta combinando con la fiscalia para poner esta casa bajo su nombre."

"No. No puede ser."

She just stared at me to say, *Sabes muy bien que todo en este país puede ser.* "He's been paying them little by little over months. Some kind of rent-to-own bullshit, no se. He's been bragging to them about it all day. In less than three weeks, we'll be his roommates, not the other way around."

"Me cago en el muy hijo de puta."

"I'm over this fucking place y su mierda," she whispered almost to herself, "He's going to make living here impossible. Tenemos que salir de aqui. Esta es la oportunidad."

"Le voy a partir la cara." Tenia una rabia encima para levantar techo.

"Lo único que vas hacer es marcharte a ese porche, and follow my lead."

"What are you going to do?"

She was halfway out of the house.

Eugenia tenia tremenda muela, and it didn't take her long to work the two over. Within fifteen minutes, the deal was made. $2000 for two days of more information. No full names, no showing our faces. Everything on the up and up.

Janaina promised, "It will respect your story, and you." Miro a Eugenia, "Te lo prometo, señora Cartas."

Made me wish Eugenia didn't have such a conscience about working with me. She would have moved product like a motherfucker.

Anibal, with his impeccable timing, walked up as money was changing hands. Aunque I stashed it rapidito, I knew he'd seen it. Motherfuckers like him see everything.

"Eh. ¿Y desde cuando ustedes son colaboradores?" he asked.

"Desde que nadie pregunto tu opinion," I said, the guy had me up to here already. Maybe it was the money, probably knowing he was trying to take the house out from under us, pero ya no me pasaba al tipo.

He spread that sly smile across his face as if warning me he had me. I walked toward him, listo para descojonarlo.

Eugenia se puso entremedio, empujandome duro hacia la puerta. "Bernardo. Un momentito, por favor."

Me le pare, watching Anibal with that fucking weasel smile. Los dos periodistas ni se movían.

"A la cocina, Bernardo. ¡Ahora!"

Fine. I walked away. Si actuaba en ese momento, alli se iba todo el dinero y cualquier oportunidad de salir de la isla.

"Perdon que te grite," she whispered in the kitchen. "Tipo es hijo de puta, but we have to just bear it until—"

De repente, en el porche se escucho tremenda griteria; Janaina. Al salir, Anibal le tiene el brazo agarrado y alandola como si la niña fuera muñeca Cabbage Patch. What's Gio doing? Fucking filming. Typical *O. Respinga.*; anything for a good story-bullshit.

Before I can stop her, Eugenia is on Anibal, pulling him by the hair down to the ground, pateandole la cara tipo Pelé.

¿Como responde el muy maricon de Anibal Cruces? En vez de tomar los golpes como todo hombre, he starts kicking his feet, como si en bicicleta, hitting Eugenia in the lower stomach.

Pipo. Allí si me empingue. Me importan tres peos las conexiones del tipo, cuantos amigos tiene en la fiscalia, o quien otro chivato del vecindario oiga el relajo. Le brinco encima a descojonarlo. Eugenia ayuda. Piñazos en la jeta por chivato. Sobre el estomago por hijo de puta. Patadas en el culo por mariconson de mierda lengua larga. Y, al fin, para estar seguro y satisfecho, me agacho y le parto la nariz. Un chorro de sangre le empapa el mentón y la quijada. El tipo grita como niña de teta hambrienta.

Janaina pulls us off as Gio tracks the camera.

"¡Apaga la fucking camara, asere!" le grito.

Janaina signals him to.

Anibal runs across the street a casa de Adira Khan, otra

chivata empedernida, screaming muffled somethings in our direction. For once, the motherfucker's mouth does not work.

They sit outside staring at the house. Within fifteen minutes, dos de la PNR vienen a pie.

"Me cago en la madre que lo pario," Eugenia whispers and then gets too loud in front of the audience that by now had gathered as close as they could get without risking being asked to talk. "¡Aqui señores! ¿Pero ya lo sabían, no?

"Señora, necesito que te calmes." It was the taller one who said it, walking a few paces in front of his partner, who was obviously a fresh rookie, stacked with fear. Anxiety splashed across his face like an Hatuey billboard.

"¡Que sorpresa!" grito Eugenia hacia Adira y Anibal. "Look who can't take care of his own shit without calling sus amigos poderosos!" Then she said to the neighborhood. "¡Dejame dejar claro lo que ya todos sabemos. Anibal Cruces es un descarado chivato acomplejado, envidioso! En quien nadie confía porque saben que tiene la lengua mas larga que una anaconda!"

"Señora, le advierto que si no bajas la voz, la llevamos a la fiscalia."

Eugenia se rió mas de la cuenta. "¿A mi? Me van a llevar a mi a la fiscalía?" She looked over at Janaina, silently prompting her to say something, tell them she'd been grabbed. La muy descarada y el camarógrafo estaban al otro lado de la calle, safely capturing it all. "Me cago en la suerta," Eugenia whispered with a chuckle. "Estaban grabando todo," she told el mas alto.

"Tienen permiso para grabar."

"Que bien. Todo muy conveniente para los extranjeros." Then, she made a very typical-Eugenia mistake: she took a couple steps toward the cops.

The rookie put his hand on his gun.

"Eugenia, no te atrevas," I said.

"Préstale atención a su marido, señora," warned the leader, now reaching for his gun.

"No es mi marido. Es mi novio. ¿Y quien carajo eres tu pa' venir a decirme lo que hacer?" She pointed across the road at Anibal, who watching it all from a safe distance, along with the rest of the neighborhood. Had we been en la Yuma, most would have been recording this drama on their phones to broadcast on evening news.

Not here. The only ones recording had permission from la fiscalia. I wondered how much longer they would be allowed to keep going.

"Señora, porque no entramos a la casa en vez de hacer esto aqui en frente del publico."

"Why? So you can do a big reveal of me in cuffs? No, do what you came to do right here and now. En frente de todas esta gente, I want you to tell me why you're arresting me and take me in."

"Eugenia, por favor, no," le rogue.

"Señor, if your wife doesn't calm down, no me va dejar mas remedio."

"¿Cuantas veces lo tengo que decir? I am not his wife."

"No grites," le advertimos yo y el alto al mismo instante.

Eugenia paró. Su cara asumiendo expresión de completa claridad. Como si de repente estuviera en paz. Este look fue seguido por la expresión que tantas veces asentó su rostro. Defiance. She felt cornered and finally knew how to get herself out; gata con uñas.

Esto terminaba tal-cual. She was taking her stance, but this was not la Yuma. The island didn't take kindly to stances.

"No estoy gritando, licenciados," she whispered to us.

El alto eased, but kept his grip on the gun handle.

With each word she took a step forward. "¡ESTO!"

El alto reached for his gun. "Señora, no des un paso mas."

"¡ES!"

"Eugenia, por favor," I whispered, esperando que a lo mejor. . .

"¡No te muevas carajo. O disparo!" dijo el alto. His partner behind him drawing the gun and aiming right at her heart.

"GRITAAAAAAAAR!"

Even I'll admit, she seemed to lunge toward them. I can't say how many shots they popped off but the noise. Me cago en diez, the fucking noise bounced up and down the street, between houses like thousands of pinball machines simultaneously hitting bonus rounds. A pesar de la bulla y el caos, solo dispararon tres balazos. Todos al medio de su pecho.

Pareció escena de Scorsese. El pecho broto tres fuentes rojizas. De manera sobrenatural, Eugenia se mantuvo de pie, miro su pecho ensangrentado, me miro fijamente, abrió la boca a decir algo, y cayo redonda al piso.

Me le acerque pero el alto pointed his gun right at my forehead. "Un paso mas y te vuelo los cesos."

Then he pointed the gun at Janaina and Gio, still filming. "Camarero," he shouted to Gio.

"Camarografo," his shocked, sheepish partner corrected him, looking at Eugenia's still body with the thousand-mile stare you might expect from a character in a yanqui war movie.

El alto didn't flinch, walking out to the street, gun pointed right at the camera. "Para de grabar. Dame la camara and cualquier notas que tengas escritas."

Janaina and Gio stayed completely calm and quiet, as if

God had hit the pause button.

El alto disparó al aire, knocking them out of their stupid, privileged, journalistically distanced gazes.

Gio handed over the camera. Janaina pulled a notepad from her back pocket. El alto asked her for any writing instruments.

"¿En donde habitan?" pregunto el alto.

They stayed quiet.

"Onde você vai ficar?!" he yelled.

"Hotel Nacional," Janaina said, lagrimas cobardes mojando sus cachetes.

"Salgan para allá. I'm going to call front desk in twenty-four hours. If you're still there, you're going to have serious problems. Understand?

They were shocked silent. For once, with nothing to say. Los traidores.

"Salpiquen."

Los dos se fueron sin el mas minimo despido, como si nunca nos habiamos conocido.

"Eugenia." No se porque la llamé, como si fuera a despertarse tan sencillamente.

"Entra a su casa, hermano. No salgas hasta que te toque la puerta."

"Eugenia," I said.

El alto apuntó a mi cara. "¿Tienes problemas de oido?"

"Entra a la casa y no salgas hasta que te toque. Si sales, te disparo. Tan sencillo."

The temptation was to walk two steps, have the fucker shoot me, and, bam, I'd be immediately reunited with Eugenia. But, no. First, I had things to do before a reunion with the love of my life.

Y como todo un pendejo, I stayed inside the house, escuchando dos policías mas llegar and hash out the story over the body. No statements were taken, no one asked my side of the story. No one in the street was questioned.

Rodillas al pecho, llorando a moco tendido con la espalda contra la pared, escuche el forense tapar el amor de mi vida, alzarla a un stretcher, y llevarsela de mi vida en ambulancia que parecía no poder transporta un tablón de sheet rock.

Me quede en ese fetal position hasta el anochecer y madrugar. Snapping out of my daze when I suddenly got cold. No preguntes como, pero a los dos de la mañana, me entro un frio del carajo. Fui al cuarto, me tapé con un hoodie, and started packing con todo lo que necesitaba to leave this place behind, never see it again.

Tenia seis botellas de keroseno. Geidy Villareal had told me to save them for her, but I wouldn't see her again. Llene el knapsack con todo el dinero y ropa que necesitaria y me lleve el butcher knife de la cocina. Le di un beso a la almohada de Eugenia and emptied three bottles of kerosene across the bed, kitchen, and living room. At the threshold of the front door, I lit it, and said goodbye to the house, my life inside it, forever.

I kicked in Adira's door. Los apuñale until they stopped screaming. Emptied the remaining three bottles of kerosene across their motionless bodies and the living room. After spitting on their corpses, I lit the gas and los mande a cagar a todos.

Caminé y llore con cojones hasta llegar cerca a la Habana, donde encontre un taxista que dijo, of course he'd take me to the airport.

"Local rate," I said.

"Dale, asere."

En cinco minutos he's talking about the craziness breaking

out all over the world. "Si más gente leyeran la biblia, el mundo seria mucho mejor."

"No me vengas con esa mierda," I snapped. "God does not exist."

He signed the cross and stayed silent the rest of the way.

When we got to the airport, I paid him double. La mejor forma de disculparme.

Securing a one-way red-eye to Miami was no problem with the cash on hand.

With unsubtle irony, the ticket agent told me to have a nice flight.

En camino a la Yuma, lloré, rezé, y mande a cagar el vacío del Mar Caribe.

En las últimas doce horas, mi vida se había hecho una plasta de mierda donde tuve que abandonar todo lo que me importaba; love, home, and country.

Eugenia me jodía que nunca rezaba. Asi que recé el vuelo entero that the plane would crash in a fiery wreck. For my sins, ninety minutes later, I landed safely in Miami.

Y aqui estaba la muy puta. . .

Que me había arruinado la vida. Wearing the same tight clothing at the hips, same long hair to just above her ass. But the difference was all over her face. Las rayas esas las conozco muy bien. Marks of guilt, sleepless nights, the haunting of events that can never be taken back. Igualita pero no la misma. Espero que haya sufrido, espero que haya trasnochado, espero que la culpa le haya. . .

"Bernardo, quiero decirte que," empezo Janaina.

"Ahora no. Ahora si que no. Vinimos a hablar business. Ustedes pueden resolver sus problemas domesticos despues. En este preciso momento, tenemos que encontrar a este hijo de puta y hacerlo arrepentir el dia que se cruzo con nosotros," dijo Ximena.

"The fuck does she have anything to do with this?" I asked the entire room.

"Whether you want to believe it or not, Mister Castillo, I have not slept since the last time I saw you."

"No lo creo. Señores Mangual, les agradezco mucho el bail, but I made myself a promise that if I ever saw this woman again, I'd kill her. And because I do not want to spend one more night in an American jail, I need to leave. Now."

Mitad de camino hacia la puerta, Ximena called out, "You

owe us, Mister Castillo."

Tomas Manguel lifted another filled glass in the air. The guy was on a mission.

"¿Cuanto fue? You'll have the money tomorrow."

"No, señor. It is not going to be that cheap. You need to help us."

"Or what?"

She smiled, walked toward me, and for the first time since coming in, pulled her glasses down so I could see her eyes. Como la mirada de Janaina, se vea que esta mujer, from international covers, exclusive interviews, and fancy red-carpet walks, had not slept since quien sabia. "There is no 'or what.' Se muy bien que nos vas a ayudar."

"¿Y como sabes eso?"

"Janaina nos dice que eres hombre de principios."

"And she's the source on who has principles and who doesn't."

"We can get this guy, Bernardo," Bailey se acerco. Her and Ximena flanking me on either side. She pulled her shirt collar, showing me donde el muy maricon de Gabe le había pegado.

"I can maybe get this guy, Bernardo," Janaina said, closing in front of me. Surrounded by three women. "With you, I know we can."

¿Que parecíamos en ese momento? Dentro de ese high-rise apartment de lujo con caras demacradas, bags under our eyes, looking like we hadn't slept desde el dia que salimos al mundo en llantos. A goddam motley crew. And I fucking hate eighties rock.

I looked past them at Tomas, who offered to pour me another.

Le brinde y tome un sip. "Bueno, señoritas, diganme. ¿Cual es el plan?"

Janaina tenia muchos defectos but one thing was sure, she was a reporter through and through. The plan was already set in motion.

We all sat around the kitchen island, drinks in hand. Tomas nodding out as they went over the plan. Janaina had already reached out to Gabe.

"Very easy, I just had to sympathize with him over the beating he received at your hands and tell him I wanted to profile him. Everything's set up. Meeting him tomorrow."

"¿Se lo creyó?"

Bailey scoffed. "Claro, el tipo solo piensa con la pinga."

"Most guys dealing with a fine female reporter do," Janaina said.

"This bitch has learned nothing. Seguro que te ha ayuda tener tremenda carrera periodística." I was going for blood. Because, fuck her.

"Me ayuda no jugar la víctima constantemente." She gulped down her drink, poured another, and drank half. "Let me tell you something, Mister Castillo. Y te lo voy a decir en español para que me entiendas claramente. Desde hace dos años, la ultima vez que te vi, no he podido dormir bien una sola noche. Sabotajé mi carrera digital por una posición inferior como escritora. No puedo mantener relaciones propias con hombres, let alone mi familia. Paré de ejercitar, pero como poco. Asi se balancea." She gulped down her drink and went to poor another, but Ximena pulled the bottle away. "Y definitivamente tomó mas de la cuenta. Asi que si tienes algo que decir, mejor decirlo ya en vez de jugar este juego de niño passive aggressive."

"Muy buen, Janaina fucking Brilhante. I will never forgive you for turning your back on me and my girlfriend when we needed you most. For being like everyone else in Cuba, una chivata que en cuanto uso lo que necesitaba, se fue corriendo como una cobarde. Y me alegro que no estes durmiendo, comiendo, cuidándote, templando.

Asi, a lo mejor, sabes, solo un poquito, por el infierno sobre el que he tenido que arrastrarme desde que tu y el camarógrafo gigantesco maricon entraron, y muy convenientemente, se escaparon de mi vida."

Janaina signed the cross. "I've never forgiven myself."

"Oh, please. Go somewhere else with that shit," I said.

"Gio se volo los sesos no mas de tres meses after that. Alone in his apartment."

"Mis mas sinceros pésames. Forgive me if I have a hard time conjuring up tears."

"Bueno, now that we've settled that. We don't have to get along, we just have to get this done," dijo Ximena.

"Me voy acostar," Tomas slurred. "Whatever you all decide has my approval. See you in the morning. Señora Cohen, Señor Castillo, mucho gusto en conocerlos."

"There's nothing to decide. Everything's already been planned out," Ximena said.

A lot may have changed en el par de años que nos habíamos visto, pero Janaina seguia bola de humo. She could still mold any room, conversation, or opportunity in her favor. Janaina explained how she was playing bruja. Enchanting Gabe with attention, piropos, and a spotlight. Telling his side of the story, casting him as the victim. Presenting his neglected perspective: stamped down by politically correct cancel culture, lynch mobs persecuting anything not progressive, woke, enlightened.

"Fuck. It's like you've been spying on him his whole life," Bailey says.

Janaina smiles. "Just took five minutes into our conversation to figure out what he's about. Like most people like him, he's not hard to decipher. I can get him to you. What's the plan after that?" she asks Bailey.

"We haven't really talked about it."

"Le vamos a partir la madre," I said.

"Asi mismo. This motherfucker needs to pay. He needs to know that when you go around acting like the world is your oyster, eventually that shell's going to clamp back down on your hand," Ximena said, pouring one last drink for everyone.

"I understand," Janaina says. "My job is the easiest. How far are you all willing to take this?"

Nos miramos unos a otros y supe, inmediatamente, que esto nos iba a unir de forma intima, mas fuerte que la belleza, el amor, sexo. Ya no era el tiempo de hable que te hable. Era tiempo de actuar. La venganza se hizo corporeal en ese high rise de lujo sobre Collins Avenue.

This is a commitment that required complete change. The hardest part of that commitment, tuning the mind to the right setting. Time to hit the gas, rev the engine, put that bitch in drive, and. . .

"Le vamos a partir la madre," dijo Ximena, sonriendo por primera vez la noche entera.

"But first I have to make him think I can knock his dick off," dijo Janaina.

"Ese hijo de puta no tiene pinga," I said.

The ladies laughed.

"He's got one all right. Unfortunately, I can confirm. He treats it like his brain, and he'll follow that little fucker around wherever it takes him," Bailey said.

"Al infierno," Ximena said. "There's no way he will join my son in heaven."

We finished our drinks, muy calladitos, until Ximena said, "Amen to that."

I, Ximena Mangual, lucked out

Internet and media trolls are right about my lack of background and training. I didn't go to Julliard, no summers at acting camp, neither one of my parents were classically trained thespians. I just fell into it. Tropece, actually. Dumb fucking luck's what helped me grasp celebrity status. All thanks to my beautiful boy, the center, anchor, of my life.

After the divorce, eran dudas constante. Whether I'd made the right decision uprooting us to Miami. Whoever honestly believes Puerto Rico is seen, considered, or treated as part of the U.S. is severely deluded. I worried Sandy'd have trouble acostumbrandose and rebel. Sandy, siendo Sandy, adapted like a chameleon. And if he didn't, I never heard about it. He complained less than me.

I always made it a point to be home when he arrived from school. Mientras que yo cocinaba, el se sentaba en la sala a terminar su homework with the TV perennially white-noising *Caso Cerrado*, a trash tabloid-reality show featuring a supposed former judge who now presided over a Spanish-language courtroom; half Jerry Springer, half People's Court. Over the end credits, a bass-heavy male voice encouraged viewers to phone in and be part of the studio audience.

"Let's go," Sandy me dijo un dia.

Impulsivo, espontaneo, simpatico. That was him.

I rolled my eyes and said sure thing. Como le hacia con muchas de sus ideas que nunca vieron la luz del dia.

Pero, tate. In a couple of weeks, we were background extras of an episode highlighting the scandalous story of a trans woman coming out to her wife while admitting to a six-year affair with her father-in-law who, at damn-near ninety, rolled out in a wheelchair and sidecar oxygen tank.

Sandy no paró su risilla durante el taping, even when I bumped his ribs after a producer whispered we had to please compose ourselves or be asked to leave.

Three taping hours went by in a finger snap. Sandy skewered these people and their universes as if he was better than all of it. Por supuesto estaba en lo cierto. Mi niño lindo was too good for this world. La única explicación por la cual Dios se lo llevara tan pronto.

On our way out, a short, stocky kid with headphones wrapping his neck stopped us to introduce himself as a Univision producer. "We spotted you in the crowd. You're beautiful," me dijo. My cheeks instantly flushed.

Sandy stepped between us. "Are you seriously hitting on my mom right now?"

Siempre feisty, como el papa. Impulsivo, espontáneo, y simpatico could work negatively too.

The producer raised his hands and stepped back. "Sorry, guys. I should have been clearer. We have a small speaking part in a telenovela we're trying to fill and we're wondering if your mom'd like to come in and read for it. Doesn't guarantee anything, but, who knows?"

Small part was being nice. Tiny, more like it. Just a couple of lines ("No se donde fue, pero si encuentras al desgraciado, llamame."). Somehow, it impressed producers and actors enough to create ripples amid the telenovela pond. That led to bigger roles, and eventually a main one, cementing me as Puerto Rico's Susan Lucci. Los tabloides le encantaban llamarme eso.

———

Este. Este momento aqui is the hardest acting gig I've ever had to pull. Reining back every urge to walk into that crowd swarming the front of the building y mandalos todos a cagar a sus madres. Out on the balcony earlier, I could only stand less than five minutes, watching them snap selfies, talking to camarografos from different outlets. They weren't there to mourn Sandy. But be seen in the moment. Agarrar sus quince minutos de fama in hopes of lucking out like me.

My curse for making it when so many others, all over the world, were trying to tread the same track, and working much harder for it. Pictures of Sandy right after he fell to earth, como el angelito que era. Blood pouring from his mouth, face split open like steaming hot Miami tarmac. A pesar de la caída y el dolor que sufrió, Sandy still tried leaving behind a smile. I could see it. Just one more moment of voluntary muscle movement, and he'd left behind a smile over his beautiful, cracked face.

They couldn't even wait twenty-four hours before showing the world su cadaver destrozado. El desgraciado culpable had to be down there. El monstruo was one of those down there clawing to be seen, off the heels of a tragedy.

I've given three years of my heart and soul for hours of their free entertainment. They couldn't give back a couple days privacy or respect.

Entra Bailey Cohen. Llorando a moco tendido en la cocina. Saying her ex-boyfriend es el monstruo desgraciado, culpable. El muy canalla, falta de respeto sent her the post despues de tremenda bronca. Y los muy hijos de puta at *O, Respinga* published it, as if they had a right.

Now I have to invoke acting skills tipo-Juilliard to tamp down la rabia telling me to grab la gringa llorona by her long, blonde ponytail and throw her full force in Sandy's same trajectory. Let the crowd snap, snap, snap and by midnight, fuacata, Bailey Cohen's dead body is the next viral sensation. Until the next exploitable tragedy strikes.

Tomas, predictably, can't keep his emotions in check. That was the second reason I left. El primero? Fucker can't stop working. Losing his family only made him dive deeper. Pobrecito. Expert at building empires. Idiot at fostering family.

I let Tomas tomar and stew until, like clockwork, he's unconscious enough to tuck into a corner and pass out. Que facil. Dios lo bendiga.

I wish I could indulge like that, pero el público me tiene entre la mirilla. Entonces. . . Muy bien. I sit patiently, listening to blubbering Bailey beg for forgiveness and an opportunity to make things right.

More acting skills cuando le digo que está perdonada. An Oscar nod as I pat her quivering hand with a momma-like there-there. Estoy tan fucking cansada, triste, y sola. "You want to make things right, Bailey Cohen?"

When Bailey's done stumbling through her story, Tomas slams his hand over the kitchen counter, takes a couple deep breaths, and reaches for the Scotch.

"How can you be with someone like that?" le pregunto.

"He wasn't like that when I knew him."

Tomas swallowed the pour like Gatorade on a hot day. "Mi cielo, everyone's like they are when we meet them."

Bailey ignores me and goes on to say su amigo fue arrestado por caerle a piñazos a Gabe. He'll help if we bail him out. "Gabe's really gotten under his skin."

"I'll do it myself," Tomas says.

"Sigue tomando," le digo.

"I have to help," Bailey says.

"Help how?" Tomas says.

"¿No estas escuchando?" I ask. Mas regaño que pregunta.

Bailey nods. "You get him out, he'll help. Trust me."

Por lo que me dice Bailey, Gabe se la pasa pensando con la pinga. And I know just like Nena to reel him in.

My girl from the Puerto Rican offices of *O, Respinga*, Janaina Brilhante, says fuck, yes she'd love an all-expense paid trip to Miami. Plus two-weeks' salary?

"Who do I have to kill?"

"All you have to do, mi amor, is pursue a story that doesn't exist."

Even in my sad, tragic, emotionally catatonic state, I manage to organize the revenge in my head. Remember, however bad people might think, I'm an actress.

By nighttime, Benardo's a free man, standing inside my living room, profusely thanking us, but apologizing for not being able to help. "Eso fue un error, atacarlo asi. He's a free man and I'm over here posting bail. ¿Para que?"

All the main players are in my living room with a plan in motion. La parte mas difícil de cualquier producción; secure a cast and have something to shoot.

Cuando le presento a Janaina por lo que creo es primera vez, Bernardo se encabrona y casi coje calle. Tomas threw plenty of tantrums back in our days. Uno mas, no me asustaba. A promise of a bigger cut of the cash later, Bernardo sigue encojonado, but listens. La parte mas difícil de cualquier producción.

Bernardo and Bailey will lay low in the condo a few days until the media circus around them dies down. Dejen que las redes se olviden un poco. Media organizations are very myopic, these days, I assure everyone.

"I hope you don't mind sleeping in Sandy's room?" les digo. It hurts but that's a tactic too, in case they start backing down or la conciencia les empieza arder. Sleeping in a recently deceased kid's room will keep them honest.

I am done acting. Especially about how good it feels, en este momento, este preciso momento, to be on the wrong side.

Estoy sumamente consciente de lo inutil que es la venganza. Aun mas consciente de que nada de esto me devolvera a mi angelito lindo.

Estoy es un pecado. Lo que estamos en proceso de planear y actualizar es puro pecado. Y, en si, es misión maternal. Dandole a mi hijo la dignidad en su vida celestial que no tuvo en su muerte terrestre.

Monstruo, salvaje, el muy hijo de puta, Gabe Acevedo, will pay for what he's done. I won't pretend there isn't satisfaction in that. I am done acting.

Who knew

getting my ass kicked would cause enough of a blip to get me internationally noticed? Bernardo Castillo stormed into the apartment like the border-hopping thug he is and beat the fuck out of me because, surprise, surprise, that's all he knows how to do. All he's good for. Hence, he spends a night in prison while I'm in a luxury high rise licking my wounds.

I should've stomped over to The Landings and smashed Bailey's face deep into the wall. Show Castillo what happens when he's in there and I'm out here. Instead, I watch her little dot on the tracking app. A red dot right across the street. A doppler radar mapping the crazy storm sweeping everyone up in its anarchic funnel.

After Castillo turned himself in to the cops like a fucking martyr, Schecter scrambled upstairs with an apology. I screamed he'd better fire that asshole pronto and slammed the door in his face.

I did one better. A call to mom and dad, next morning Schecter's out of there. Who the fuck cares? That'll teach him.

Turns out, I'm on unofficial house arrest. What with The Landings and Las Brisas being the media hotspots they are these last couple of days. When I went downstairs to the mailboxes and peeked outside the windows, photographers snapped away at an attention-craving mob.

Local media's camped out day and night, spinning this into some sort of movie of the week.

Bernardo Castillo's myth and lore gain some traction after his bail's taken care of by the grieving parents. He's painted an immigrant folk hero fighting the good fight on behalf of privacy, respect for life, and overall morality.

I, who took the pictures, am, of course, the heavy.

Elias is the hippie with a conscious. The dumb fuck who opened his mouth. "Yeah, he's kinda of a weird dude. I noticed that from the jump, so I just stayed away. You know when you just instantly click with some people? Didn't happen between me and him. He was always self-absorbed, and I don't have time to bring that kind of energy into my life," he told the evening news.

What-fucking-ever. Guy has no stake in my life.

One guy who does at the moment, and peddles in unconscionable behavior, also seems to have let guilt skitter around in his brain. Pablo Porras is desperate to get off the phone, saying he's "muito ocupado."

I remind the Brazilian nut I've got exactly what he's looking for. Nitty-gritty, up-close, and personal access to the story nobody else can get. "What side of the story do you want to be on here, irmão?"

"Nah, nah. That story is dead in the water. We need to keep our content fresh. Besides, honestly, no one wants to hear your side of it. It's the other guy everyone wants. Castillo. He's the man in the iron mask. You're just the guy getting his ass kicked. How's your face, by the way? Cos from the looks of the images, IR-mão. . ."

"You motherfucking, soccer-kicking, linguiça-eating piece of shit, if I ever make it down there, I swear to God. . ."

Pablo Porras laughs maniacally, then catches his breath. "See? That's the kind of shit I'm looking for. Got you all on record, too. Tell you what, irmão, you make it down here, alive, to our offices, the caipirinhas are on me."

Click.

Goddam filho da puta.

He's not wrong, though. Local news only want to hear Bernardo's side. As if he's the victim. Like he's the one sitting home with his bottom lip split open like an overheated salchicha, right-eye, from the temple down, half shut.

Bernardo Castillo resides and works here illegally. Is arrested after breaking into a resident's apartment of the luxury high rise he works in to commit serious assault and battery, and jailed. To be hailed a hero in the end. Only in butt fuck, ass-backwards America.

When do I get the microphone? Show the world Bernardo, Bailey, the kid, his mildly famous mother, this entire fucking production, is putting law breakers, moochers, and celebrity fuckers on a fifteen-minute pedestal.

The cesspool of Collins Avenue is asses to ankles with people dying to be seen. They don't care about the kid or his family. All they want is to impress their friends with a picture on NPR or a quote on late night news. Something to look back on down the line, celebrate better days.

I shut off the TV and harken my inner Bailey by killing a bottle of wine. If the world is going to keep me imprisoned twenty-plus stories above Miami Beach, might as well uncork one of the cunt's favorite reds. Drinking with spite is empowering. Halfway down the bottle, feelings of apathy and disassociation grow warm inside. Out on the balcony, looking down on the crowd, I spit. The wind makes a kite of the tiny wad, blowing it out to sea. I tilt the bottle and bless the masses. Most of it blows away too, but some seems to trickle down over the bandwagon. Some idiots wipe their damp heads and look up, clueless.

"You really shouldn't do that." Sheldon, the next door neighbor—who loves to stick his giant nose where it doesn't belong—says, peeking out from his own balcony.

"Get the fuck inside, old man."

"Last I checked this was a free country."

"Then let me live my life before I walk over there and shove this bottle sideways up your tuchus."

"That's why the news is all over you, son."

I raise the bottle aiming right at his Pinocchio nose. If I throw just right, it'll break in two. He gasps and scrambles inside.

My phone rings. Area code 787. It's been blown up the last couple of days by reporters and prank callers, mostly fans of Mangual cursing me out in native languages I don't understand but have lived here long enough to get the gist.

The alcohol rage boiling inside me is about to make this tirade epic. Play this shit back on your news clip, assholes.

"How can I make your day a living hell?" I say.

"Hello. I'm sorry. . . I'm trying to reach Gabriel Acevedo."

"It's Gabe." I snap. But, stop the presses. Whoever this is sounds cute as hell. Her English is clipped with an accent peppered by a hit of ghetto lilt.

"This is him. Sorry. The last couple of days have been anarchy when it comes to answering this phone.

"I can imagine."

She's definitely Spanish. I can listen to that accent all day.

"My name is Janaina Brilhante. I'm a reporter with *O, Respinga*."

"No way, lady. If this is some kind of joke on Pablo Porras' part, you can tell him to suck my . . ."

"No, no, Mister Acevedo. I work at the Puerto Rican offices. I've only reached out to Mister Porras as a contact point. He said I could do what I want. He feels the story is dead in the water."

"Listen, I'm already getting shit on, on the daily. I don't need an—"

"Mister Acevedo. Just give me a moment to explain. In my research, I've noticed a close connection between your story and the Mangual family. You know who they are?"

"Of course."

"Would I be wrong in my assumptions about their close connection to this story?"

"Not at all, señorita. Para nada."

"Perfect. Then, you know they're huge here on the island. I just pitched my editors an idea to come out there and get the other side of the story. Your side."

"The side no one wants to hear?"

"Yes. Absolutely. I'd like to get your side of the story that, in my humble opinion, has been severely neglected. Someone breaks into your house, violently attacks you, and somehow you're the villain."

Wow. Is she an angel come down from heaven? "Janaina. Such a beautiful name."

"Thank you," she says with a giggle. "So, is this something you'd be interested in? It would just be a few days, three tops. And that's a max. The idea is to sit down and get a good, wide understanding of what's happening from your vantage point. I'm interested in getting disenfranchised sides of the story. Of course, we'd pay you for your troubles."

"How much?"

"I'll talk to my editors soon as we hang up. Don't expect to retire on it."

"How does this work? Do you stay here with me?" Worth a shot.

"Ugghh. . . No, Mister Acevedo. I'd be staying on my own and all our face-to-face interactions would take place in public."

She doesn't sound offended. Maybe, just maybe, it sounds like she's okay with the idea. "Of course. I know. I'm sorry. I don't know why I said that."

"It's okay, Mister Acevedo. Give me just a short time and I'll get back in touch with all the details."

"Yes. I'll be here. Thanks so much, Janaina. I'll await your call."

"No problem, Mister Acevedo."

I walk to the railing, peering over. It's after work hours and more leeches have gathered to show their support for the dead boy. More cops phalanx the front entrance of The Landings. Photographers snap their pictures while behind them the crowd chants Sandy's name.

What fucking luck. A sexy-ass voice comes offering a new opportunity at cash and some justice in the court of public opinion. There is a God. Her name is Janaina, and she speaks English spiced with some Spanish ghetto sazón. She's coming to my home turf, to interview and make me the central focus. If there's a merciful God, her brown legs will be wrapped around my neck soon.

I raise the bottle like a sacramental offering to my new God and the temple of her holy pussy, saluting my ability to hustle and weasel my way forward. "Here's to Bernardo Castillo still in jail, to Bailey Cohen, a blip on my phone. Here's to Gabe Acevedo, up here over all of them, paid for his say."

I swallow down a couple of large gulps then tip the bottle over the railing, consecrating the crowd.

When Janaina calls back a little over an hour later, I'm floating so free, I barely talk so she won't hear my slurred speech. Says she'll be here tomorrow afternoon with five grand. Way more than I expected.

Life is good. I'm back in business. I finish the rest of the bottle in one long pull.

Next day, I'm nursing a nasty hangover, but way too excited about la Boricua who's fine culo is seeking my undivided attention. Yuuuuummyy.

During her confirmation call, she sounded gooey-excited to be in Miami.

"I've lived in Miami my entire life. Make a great tour guide if you have the time."

"I have the time, Mister Acevedo, but I am afraid accepting such an offer could present a conflict of interest if you do understand. Nothing personal, strictly professional."

"I understand." With nothing to lose, I knew with just a bit more effort and patience, I'd get her alone with in no time, with no problem.

"Great. Also understand, I'm working here and need to hit the ground running," she says. "I've only got four days with you, so we need to make the most of it. You'll be begging me to leave by the end of it, believe me."

That little ghetto twang makes her coy and cute and me so goddam caliente. What I will be begging for is a taste of her muy sabroso cinnamon roll.

"What's a good place to meet?" she asks. "I'm on the beach, so we're close."

I can't help but think she's purposely emphasizing our proximity should I want to play later. "News Cafe. Know where it is?"

"No. Why don't I come to your place, and we go from there."

There it is. Although she insists on meeting in the lobby, it's a first step in the right direction. If she's as loosey-goosey as she sounds on the phone, then it's going to be a good night.

And so, I must do my best: look good, smell good, sound good. Give Janaina Brilhante a story that wraps her so tight it jabs her between the ears and moistens between her legs.

She's all business. The moment we settle in the ride-share down to South Beach, the digital recorder comes out. "You mind? It helps me later in case I miss anything in my notes."

"Of course not. Do what you need to do."

"Beautiful. Tell me about this odyssey with Bernardo Castillo."

My stomach tightens at the spic's name.

By the end of the car ride, I'm on the chapter about Bailey's drinking and overall laziness.

After splitting the ceviche appetizer, Janaina can't stop raving how good it is. I'm hoping the rumors about seafood and sex drives are true.

Perfect time to amp up the vulnerability. "Next day, I'm turning into my building, fucking body falls out of the sky."

Her eyes widen. She orders a mojito (hopefully she'll be later) and the grilled portobello entree. She's enraptured, so I just keep talking without her having to ask questions. There's a flair in her eyes I never saw in Bailey.

The flair of drive and confidence that exist from knowing what she's doing, being good at something. Only professionals have that flair. Here's a mamita who knows what she wants from life, how to grab after it. Gulping down the rest of my red, I say, "Bailey could do well in talking to you."

"Sorry?"

"Nevermind. Just thinking out loud."

Why the fuck did I mention that bitch? My refill comes with impeccable timing.

As the night goes on, dessert's skipped and she's fascinated as I've taken extra care to highlight the bits that make me a badass. Having Bernardo fired, telling Pablo Porras to go fuck himself. She doesn't mention the pictures and neither do I.

"Time for one more drink?" she asks. "This is really good stuff."

"So, Bernardo is fired, and he comes knocking on your door," she continues. All business.

"Yup. To beat the fuck out of me like a wild animal."

"No one heard or saw anything?"

"No one claimed to, but I got all that shit on tape."

"There's video?"

Gabe taps on the table. "What the fuck is taking these. . ." A server crosses the floor. "Oye, Paco. Can I get another glass, please? My throat's dry as a nun's. . ." Janaina's eyeballing me. Must relax. "Can I have another glass?"

The server forces a smile. "My name's Steven, sir. I'm not your server but I'll be glad to assist. What were you drinking?"

"The Mad Servant pinot. Make it a double, please."

"Coming right up."

Janaina flicked her eyebrows and cleared her throat.

"Sorry," I say. "Sometimes with wait staff, you just have to."

"It's fine. Back to business. You were saying there is video of the attack."

"Yup. Multiple angles. Mounted a camera on my front door and got two looking into my living room. I held on to the footage because I know he's a poor fucking immigrant who'd probably get kicked out of the country for assaulting an American. No offense."

"None taken. I'm not an immigrant. I'm from Brazil with a work visa."

"Brazil? I thought Puerto Rican."

She flicked her pinky in the air. "You need to learn your accents, Mister Acevedo. She clears her throat again and writes furiously in her pad. "Would you be willing to extend this little interview to show me that footage? Just, you know, to get as much well-rounded information as I can."

"Yeah. Thing is, it's back at my place."

Testing the waters.

"I figured."

"You're okay with that?"

"Wouldn't suggest it if I wasn't." She drinks her last mojito in one go, tapping the rim of the empty glass with a long acrylic nail I imagine tickling the tip of my cock. "Will you be able to top me off?"

"I don't have stuff to make mojitos, but there is a shit ton of wine."

"Let's hit it."

I get the check and we're out of there.

In the car, it takes a monk's willpower to not run my hand's up her brown thighs. Back home, I pop a cork of pinot noir, pour two tall-ass glasses, and click through the surveillance camera cloud.

Janaina's luscious ass looks likes two full packs of flour as she shuffles close to me on the couch for a better look. I want to bend and bite down on her like an Olympic finalist on the podium as the anthem blares across the venue.

"Jesus," she says. Her eyes brightened by the reflection of the video. "He charged in here like a pro wrestler."

"Guy's a fucking devil."

She clears her throat. She keeps watching me on video, crawling on the floor away from my attacker. Bernardo had kicked my ribs and I remember having trouble breathing at that point. This footage is embarrassing. I wish I hadn't agreed to showing it. Makes me look like a bitch; slowly, pathetically, squirming away. At one point, Bernardo kicks me right between the ass cheeks, sending me face down on the floor like a star fish.

Janaina chuckles but tries masking it by sipping wine.

Who, the fuck, does this bitch think she is?

She tries playing it off by writing some shit into her notebook as Bernardo Castillo fucks me up a bit more before walking off frame. Now I'm close up, battered and bleeding on the floor like a stuck pig. Through tears, I look right into the lens and whimper, "Please help."

Jesus Christ. I'd forgotten that. Who was I reaching out to?

"All right, that's about it. I think you got more than you needed."

Janaina holds up her half-full wine glass, a non-verbal cue she wants to stay.

"It's been a long ass-day and I'm tired. We'll have more time tomorrow."

Janaina downs the rest of her wine. "Same time?"

"Yeah. Where?" I stand and start for the door.

Who gives a fuck about this bitch? I'm pissed I gave into

her bullshit. What did I expect from a Puerto Rican? Brazilian, wherever the fuck she's from. All the same pile.

"News Cafe. I really liked their ceviche."

"Fine."

"Want me to come here first?"

"Nah. Let's meet there."

"Okay. Is something wrong? I feel there's something you're not telling me."

"As the professional reporter you claim to be, you always go around laughing at people you interview?"

"I wasn't laughing at you. I swear. This is all very shocking. I'm one of those people who laughs when they're nervous. Makes me very unpopular at funerals."

"Sounds like a great story."

"I'll see you tomorrow?"

"Yup. Same time."

I close the door on her face. Let the flimsy cunt find her own way out.

———————

Almost an hour later, I power drive through a third glass of wine, scanning the night's footage. Freezing on a masterpiece of a screenshot where Janaina bent down to pick up a napkin she'd dropped. That small, brown cleavage lay bare just for me. Her tits are disproportionate to her ass. Most of the jelly went to the back. I whack it to her and she's none the wiser.

My balls are drained and my head light when the phone buzzes. The caller ID flashes: *JANAINA BRILHANTE*.

"I'm so glad you answered," she says.

I'll entertain the game. "Why wouldn't I?"

"It was fucked up of me to laugh at you. Just, honestly, I didn't expect the footage to be so in my face. It made me nervous. You're very courageous to talk to me about it. I really appreciate you doing this favor for me. It's huge."

"That was a bad reaction on my part. It's just the second time I watched the footage myself. Just pisses me off what the guy did to me."

Right on. Get her feeling sorry for him.

"I feel bad, which is why I called my bosses to see if we can offer you a little more incentive for what you're doing. They love my notes so far. They're toying with the idea of a docuseries with you as the focus. They're going to pay you a lot more if it gets picked up. They haven't said exactly how much but at least four times."

"Fuck yes," I say. Fucking finally.

Janaina laughs. "Good. I thought it might take a little more convincing."

"Not at that price."

"Great, so they want us all to meet tomorrow at the *O, Respinga* office in Downtown."

"There's an office here?"

"We have offices everywhere, a lot of people don't know about."

"Okay. Meet there?" I ask.

"I'll come pick you up and we'll ride together," she says.

"No dinner?" I ramp up the disappointed tone.

"That's why we're riding together. I figure we could celebrate after conducting business."

"I should be paying you for the honor." The offer of more money has made me brazen.

"The pleasure is all mine, Gabe Acevedo. I'll call tomorrow

when I'm on my way."

"Can't wait."

I walk to the bedroom clutching the wine bottle and take a long swig like a fucking general. Giddy, drunk, I roll on the floor, laughing just like when. . . Fuck. There's never been another time I've been this happy.

We're actually talking about it.

Conspiring voices confirm and finalize the plot in a whirring background buzz as I look across the street to Las Brisas. Gabe's window is closed. Has been the last two days. Why the fuck do I keep checking?

I'm listening but there's a persistent hum in my ears. Like I'm stuck inside a tunnel with a persistent buzz. Might be my conscience, Amaury Sambrano tapping my shoulder from beyond the grave, nudging me forward, yelling at me to quit acting like such a scared baby.

I ticked all the boxes after high school. College, check. Bachelor's degree, check. Moving out of my folks', check. Established independence, check. Nothing shook Amaury's ghost off my back.

I had a good gig on my own. A steady part-time in the evenings while I built a client list during the day. A small efficiency way out west, a stone's throw from The Miccosukee reservation. I loved it, every night crossing from the glitz and glamor of the beach to settle in The Everglades' quiet swampiness.

It was beautiful to be so busy, so far away from hubbub to have time for much else. Then, Clarissa and Hannah forced me out on a rare Friday when I could muster the energy. It was at South Beach's Purdy Lounge I met Gabe. A month later, I'd crossed back over the superficial border to live and hustle on South Beach. And that's where I became complacent and comfortable enough to let Gabe get comfortable enough to mess with my mind, to delude me into believing his taunting and subtle jokes about my career path and overall outlook on life came from a place of care and vigilance.

A second Bailey was born then, South Beach Bailey. The first Bailey—old me, sitting outside the efficiency to watch that beautiful sun set over the green patchwork of The Everglades, cold beer in hand, smile on my face from the contentment of a hard day's hustle—would have smacked South Beach Bailey across the face, called her a dependent bitch, yelled at her to get her shit together.

That persistent hum isn't a tunnel. It's a cacophony of voices past. Ones I let down time and again, saying, *Fucking finally. Look who has her shit together!*

It's neither old nor new Bailey inside this high rise now, listening to the Manguals, Bernardo, and the cute journalist talking about it without saying it, like it's, as Bernardo might say, mala leche.

"We're going to kill him," I say, almost to myself.

The buzz stops and they turn to me as if they don't know what I'm talking about, but they do. Every other person inside that condo, high up above the tumult below on Collins, knows exactly what's being talked about here, so I talk about it. I know what I'm saying. Tomas and Ximena Mangual know what I'm saying.

Removing someone from existence. Playing God. This won't bond us; it will fucking fuse us together. Partners for life. I'm okay with that after a life that's done not much more than take, take, take.

Once this is done, original Bailey will reemerge. I like her. She gets her hands dirty. Knows, deep in her bones, that Gabe deserves to pay, that Sandy and his parents deserve to be avenged, that she and Bernardo deserve a chance at a better life. This is the Bailey who has not had, or felt the need for, a drink since the tragedy.

The Manguals agree on a million each. More than enough to start over as the original.

That night, me and Bernardo talk to each other in the dark of Sandy's room. It's not as haunting as I thought it might be.

"Es una idea solida. Con el dinero, tu y yo nos podemos ir de aqui. Empezar una vida nueva," Bernardo says.

"¿Where? Cuba?" I say the most absurd thing that comes to mind because it's what the moment calls for.

Bernardo laughs. He hasn't been the same since after fucking up Gabe. I get it. The guy does that to anyone who hovers in his general direction. It woke a darkness in Bernardo I suspected was there because who's not carrying around a little blackness in them. Something in his eyes hasn't been the same. They don't focus like before. His shoulders have been tense all night; he shifts them around like carrying a heavy backpack. The most off I've ever seen him. Carrying his own demon, his own ghost.

"Mas nunca vuelvo a ese lugar."

Cuba's to Bernardo what Miami's become for me, repellant. "Bueno," I say. "Dime tu. ¿A dónde quieres ir?"

He looks out the window at the ocean, palms, and buildings. A sliver of a smile cuts across his face. "Puerto Rico. We can get lost over there."

"Bien. Pero antes del retiro viene el trabajo."

Everything's in motion.

Bernardo's been nervous staying in Sandy's room, sleeping on the floor every night.

"Relajate, Bernardo. Nada te va a pasar. A de mas," I flex her arm. "Yo te protejo."

"No te rias de los muertos."

I offer him a spot on the bed. He refuses, turning his back.

Instead of sleep, I lie staring at the ceiling. Sandy's Mangual's ghost hovering around the room, blowing my hair back, tickling my toes. Amaury Sambrano's ghost is in there too. Clear as a campana, I hear that voice, too fabulous for whoever heard it. I cry to the cacophony of voices. Nothing gets me to sleep.

———————

Fine, maybe I am a little jealous of Janaina Brilhante. I mean, firecracker comes in out of nowhere, all Brazilian fizz and pop, and all of a sudden this idea that was mine becomes everyone's. Her and Bernardo have history. He won't tell me what, but it goes back to Cuba and we don't talk about Cuba, no, no, no.

I've never seen Bernardo as encojonado as when he saw her standing in the Mangual's living room. He's a prideful person and was already uncomfortable owing his freedom to others, especially people he considered privilegiados. I know he's pissed about the way I strongarmed him into this. Same time, Gabe needs to pay for being Gabe.

Ximena promised to set the plan in motion, which requires Miss Rio standing in the living room, promising to volley Gabe so we can spike him. I'll give it to her, she's willing to put herself out there with the fucker to get him closer to us.

What a shocker when she comes back from their first encounter horrorizada.

"Que paso?" Ximena says.

"I need a glass of wine."

Ximena pours three tall glasses of pinot grigio for the ladies. The men wave the offer away, rapt with attention.

Janaina takes a long pull then asks me, "How the fuck could you stand that guy so long? Christ, he's repulsive. I could feel his eyes all over me when my back was turned. His creep numbers are off the Richter Scale. We might have a problem, though."

"¿Que paso?"

"He was showing me the surveillance video of you kicking his ass and I lost it when you literally kicked him in the ass," she says to Bernardo. "Tried holding it in but he heard me giggle."

Ximena sighs deep. "Jana, como se te ocurre?"

"Sorry, but." She holds her glass up at Bernardo. "De verdad que lo jodiste todo. Like the good old days."

Bernardo stood up and walked toward her, like he might do something. So convincingly that Ximena stepped in front of me. He smiled down at her. "I'm not going to touch her. La ultima vez que yo vi a esta mujer, she was watching while my life was ripped to shit and did nothing to try and assist me or the ones I cared for. That's the type of trash you're dealing with, Señora Mangual."

As Bernardo walks past him en route to the bedroom, Tomas offers him a drink. Benardo waves it away.

"I swear to God I'm doing this for him."

"He won't realize it until much later. And that's a big maybe. Anyway. . . you laughed at Gabe, who's super sensitive." Bailey says. "He can't stand that kind of attention. Good job."

"Hey, you want to be the one to try it? I'll gladly switch spots with you any day. Oh, wait, you're the jilted ex."

"Bitch, you want I should fuck you up right now?" I stood so hard, so fast, the bar chair I was on slammed back against the floor.

Ximena slammed her fist down on the kitchen island top.

"Will you two shut the fuck up so I can listen? We have more important things to worry about. We don't have time for a stupid cat fight."

"Anyway," Janaina eyeballed me hard. His mood changed like that." Janaina snapped her fingers. "I tried to coo him at the end with a promise of dinner, but he shooed me out of there and refused to walk me down. I mean his ego was fucking butt hurt."

"He totally would be," I said. "Was he drinking?"

"Yup."

"Knowing him, he still is. Call him back and talk nice. He'll meet up again."

Ximena nods her head. "Llamalo, pide disculpa. Make it sound like you really feel bad about all this and get back in his good graces."

Janaina takes in a big breath, lets it out slow, then smiles at me. "What's his weakness?"

"Money's no guarantee," Bailey says. "Gabe craves attention more than anything. More than money."

"Maybe we can. . ." Ximena starts.

Janaina shushes her. "Everybody, please, calladitos, so I can think."

She walks into the shadows of one of the hallways—quirky broad—and comes back with an empty wineglass. Without hesitation, she picks up the phone.

Flirting, giggling, twirling her hair, raising and lowering her voice for effect. Esta nena is pure method. Before she hangs up and smiles at us, I know he's taken the bait.

God damn, she's good. Maybe even growing on me a bit. They're meeting tomorrow, she says with a smile and the thought of Gabe walking right into the plan center stage has got me giddier than ever.

So much so, I walk to the kitchen for a whiskey. I take water from the cooler instead. "Bueno, mi gente." I hold up my glass. "Let's toast to the memory of Sandy Mangual, who's brought us together in the name of vengeance." It's the first time I've said his name in the last few days without bursting into tears.

After a toast, we leave Tomas at the apartment and the rest of us drive out to Bernardo's efficiency. Ximena's got the homeowners gushing seconds after meeting them. "Una actriz tan famosa y talentosa en nuestra casa,"

Ximena's not acting as she speaks to them quietly, honestly. She wants the house for twenty-four hours. All they have to do is leave early tomorrow morning and stay gone twenty-four hours. In exchange, two years' worth of Bernardo's rent, cash, and a promise to God to return the place in the exact same condition it's received. No questions asked, however. Complete confidentiality. By the end of it, the sextagenarians are in quiet cahoots.

As we leave, the old man shouts out to Ximena, sheepishly asking for a picture. Of course. The couple's night is made.

The following morning, the house is empty as promised. Ximena goes from actress to director as we practice our spots and roles for Gabe's big arrival. Tomas is a quick study despite a vicious hangover. The porch and backyard lights are removed to reduce visibility.

Actors take their positions, house lights dim, and the back of stage prepares for the one night only premiere of Teatro Venganza, a production of Karmic Occurrences. Adults only. The audience is warned: some of the action depicted may be very graphic and disturbing.

I didn't give a fuck

I didn't give a shit if I looked like I ran a mile in under eight minutes, or if I ballooned mere months before prom. Not like I had a date anyway. In turn, no one at Saint Ignatius cared for me, so why keep myself from doing what I loved? Which, in high school, was mostly eating. Eating and studying.

I didn't try to be a social pariah, believe me. I was as sociable as they come with no reason to be ornery. Parents were still together, didn't smack me around, and my GPA meant a full ride to the University of Florida. Senior year, I was ready to get my diploma and give Saint Ignatius Catholic High School an erect, bony finger. Mom and dad mostly left me alone as long as I stayed focused and kept my grades up. It was a sweet life. No reason to complain or worry about superficial shit.

Believe it or not, this outlook actually made me uber nice. To everyone. Which was a problem. In those years, where high school rebellion and teenaged angst were all the rage, it didn't make me a popular classmate. Even in a $15,000/year institution—I'm willing to bet because of it—the kids had no problem letting me know how out of favor I was.

Granted, my resume didn't help. You know the drill. Class

president, National Merit Scholar, honors society. I was the girl who finished her service hours a year in advance. Who the guidance counselor, Ms. Hickey, blasted her UF admission across the school PA. Perfect attendance, not a day missed. If I was sick, dad would wait until I was marked present to pull me out early.

Eye rolling and teeth sucking abounded when I came in the room, so I had to cope. And food was my fucking guru. Kept me focused, honest, with a keen eye on making sure I got into university, into a world operating away from cliques, idiotic rivalries, and high school sports statistics. Hit the ground running on a fast track to a four-year degree. My plan was to get that bitch done in just under three.

Among high school bitches, Leeza Cifuentes was a C-U-N-T.

She turned seventeen at the start of senior year and marked it with an open house rager whose guest list ran across three schools. Everyone and their mothers except, guess who? Which would have been fine except Leeza did not possess quiet dignity. So post-party Monday, Leeza and her two minions, Arianna Viasco and Johanna Carrascal, reminded the whole school about the only senior not in attendance.

The teasing overshadowed my winning the National Book Award and a UF scholarship that same week. Mom and dad came through, treating me to a feast at my favorite Italian spot, Salvatore D's. In between the calamari fritti and gnocchi samantha, dad ordered two glasses of red wine. Mom didn't drink. With a sneaky smile and a wink, he said, "Bottoms up."

Mom, usually a ball buster, said, in conspiratorial whisper, "Just one." Then directly to dad, "Don't make this a thing."

The wine warmed my stomach and the food made me smile. Who needed friends when I had accolades?

The three whores had incredible bodies, which for them made changing after gym class a non-issue. Coach Valerie didn't give a shit unless teachers complained about odors. I was always locked and cocked with body sprays and plenty of deodorant.

The girls' taunting was relentless. Mind you, I'd only take my shirt off for the thirty seconds it took to switch from one to the other. *Did anyone order raw dough from the bakery? Who thought it was possible to have love handles bigger than your titties? The cafeteria won't have a run on ham.*

It never got physical so I ignored them. I had mad resilience.

Coach Valerie wasn't so patient, cornering the three girls after a particularly vicious taunting session and hitting them with a week's worth of afterschool detention. She then took me into her office and said a good person doesn't deserve this "bullshit" on senior year.

"I need to fulfill my physical education credit. I pushed it off to the end," I said.

"I'll talk to the office. You'll swap to another elective and have it count just the same."

"Is that the right thing to do?"

Coach Valerie smiled. "Those bitches doing the right thing?"

Leeza, Arianna, and Johanna used their week in detention to ramp up the ire and come at me with a vengeance.

My spot at lunch was an outdoor table at the farthest corner from the buzzing cafeteria hive. Some would call it sad; I called it paradise. Halfway into a slice of cold cheese pizza, browsing the syllabus for my new history of film elective, a fabulous voice from behind broke the air.

"May I?"

Pow! In comparison to other boys at Saint Ignatius, here stood a man. Light-post tall, unblemished olive skin clearly maintained by a treatment regimen to rival the queen bees'. Tight black curls dangling and swinging like vermicelli over two gemstone eyes shining Sicilian sea-water blue.

"Of course." I nervously slid over, making enough berth for a shipping container.

"You're in Lightfoot's film class," he said. "And you just left without introducing yourself. What's up with that?"

"I was just sitting in. I'm switching electives, trying to see which class interests me before making a decision."

"You realize I'm the only one in that class? So, when you just get up and walk away it's, like, super rude."

He amplified the femininity in his voice so the *rude* came out as a sharp, snarky exclamation mark.

How God damn cute.

"Sorry. I didn't want to make it awkward if I ended up deciding not to attend."

He held out a dainty hand. "Amaury Sambrano. You, my socialite?"

"Bailey Cohen."

"Well, aren't you cut from the all-American cloth?"

"My mom's Cuban."

"Keep that to yourself, honey. Newsflash: you're in that film class, I'm in that film class. Hence, there's no way in hell you're getting out of it. Você entende?"

"Brazil?" I asked.

He nodded.

"You should probably keep *that* to yourself," I whipped back.

His laugh filled the breezeway. Not caring who heard him or might be uncomfortable by the sound of his joy, a man after my heart. "I like you, Bailey Cohen. There might be hope for this cesspool of a school yet."

Amaury filled the next fifteen minutes talking like he'd known me for years. Said he hadn't a wink of sleep the night before. First time in a Catholic school. "A fabulous gay icon like me."

Of course he'd be gay. Quality man like that. I harbored many things. A crush would be just another added to the pile. Oh, well.

Amaury made devil horns with his index and pinkie finger and planted them over his forehead. "Want to be friends with the devil?"

"Yes, I do," I said through giggles.

The bitch trio walked toward us with Leeza glaring daggers.

Without missing a beat, Amaury turned and, still playing devil, snapped, "Your mother sucks cocks in hell."

It was the first time I'd ever seen them left with nothing to say.

Amaury continued staring as they walked on, as if fixing a hex into their vertexes. "Cunts," he said to me. "You're not one. Are you, Bailey?"

"I don't think so."

"Good answer. Shows you aren't one. Don't ever become one or I'll drop you like this."

He snapped his fingers, and I was over the moon.

We left our first film class together thick as thieves and each harboring intense crushes.

One class period is all it took for me to become wrapped up in Amaury's entire universe, strangle-held by his confidence. There was no fear in the man as he navigated the very narrow-minded Saint Ignatius hallways. The type of anomaly popular kids are too intimidated by to even attempt to decipher. By seventeen, he navigated a world his own. Weapons at his disposal? Outspokenness, direct eye contact, and a sharp tongue that quickly slit any hater's throat. I'd watch Amaury Sambrano make breakfast. Finally, something tangible and real to consume me. Obsession, here I came.

Mister Lightfoot floored Amaury just as quick. The fifty minutes of film class was the only block of time my extroverted friend was stone quiet, to later gush about his sense of style, how he never needed notes during his lectures. "It all just pours from his fountain of intellect through those lips ripe for kissing. Thank God it's just us two in there because I'd hate to share the love of my life."

He didn't have to worry about me being attracted to anyone else, and we were inseparable. He walked me to class even if it was out of his way and was marked tardy next period. We studied together; my house one week, his the other. Both sets of parents pleased as Planter's Punch to have their children functioning outside their norm of isolation. Not like we needed it. We were both sharp as tacks, so most of the time was reserved for hanging out and Amaury helping me sharpen my social game ever so slightly. Together, we were a motley fucking crew.

To catch Lightfoot's attention, Amaury altered his school uniform so it was tight as chainmail, hugging every curve on that bunda linda. He'd pepper Portuguese into our class discussions. So charming.

Of course, as all good, misunderstood things go, Saint Ignatius boys ramped up their taunting. Blowing kisses, dainty whistles, and homophobic slurs tossed about as we, the "queer caravan," passed through the hallways. That was Amaury's nickname for us. Shit like that didn't bother him at all. Where most boys his height might slouch to avoid attention, Amaury stood erect and steady like an old oak.

He helped me lose weight. We exercised every day, and he taught me to eat properly. It was a struggle the first few weeks eliminating sugar and salts, especially when tests loomed around. The first pounds proved the hardest and most worthwhile. As pounds dropped, my confidence rose. The addiction to that confidence was instant. My walk became a little taller, like Amaury's. When he told me I was "ready," then came the makeover. Goodbye glasses, hello contacts.

"Eyeliner's a must and, for God's sake, stop wearing plaid." He signed the cross and got to work on my makeup. "Those three bitches would kill for almond-shaped eyes like yours. Make those things pop, girl. You've also got killer tits, but no one can see them with that goddam parachute hoodie you walk around with."

"I'm trying to hide them," I said.

He arched like he might back-bend. "Tits and teeth, baby. Most of life is about tits and teeth."

Our mutual crushes grew in tandem.

With Homecoming around the corner, I'd shed fifteen pounds and the student body noticed. Looking so good, girls still rolled their eyes at me, but now out of envy.

Lightfoot's class became our Shangri-La, breezing through the curriculum and using the loads of free time to gossip about the student body, staff, and parents. Lightfoot was fresh out of academia and admitted relief at landing such an amazing class.

"You'll never get two charmers like us in the same room at once, I promise you that. This pairing only happens once every

Halley's Comet," Amaury assured.

By Winter Formal, we were the pair Saint Ignatius loved to hate. Amaury's fashion sense put all the boys to shame and turned more than a few of the senior girls' heads. I was twenty-five pounds lighter, and my tits got all the eyeballs soon as I walked into the room. This dance was the last hooray before winter break, during which we'd planned to ramp up the health routine. Come back to campus the school's answer to Brangelina.

I rocked a teal seafoam mermaid cut. Amaury was in a matching slim fit suit that looked fresh off a Parisian runway. Mom almost made us late snapping so many pictures.

A lot of our study sessions turned into impromptu dancing. We owned that goddam dance floor with teachers and students alike watching us.

"Lightfoot keeps staring at me," Amaury whispered at one point.

"Everyone is," I said.

An hour in, Amaury said he needed to use the bathroom.

Perfect. I perched by the refreshment table to cool down. I couldn't tell you what it was that sent every single creep at that dance trying to swoon me with some of the most obvious, most disgusting, pick-up lines in the history of oral communication.

After the fourth creeper hurled a pickup line that Ted Bundy would whip his head at, I got antsy, and wanted back out on the dance floor with the unrequited love of my life. Back to making the queen bees jealous.

Amaury had not responded to the text message I'd sent fifteen minutes earlier. We'd sipped a bit of celebratory wine back at the house, but he'd used the bathroom before leaving. The fuck was taking him so long?

I killed some time in the bathroom stall and took the long way back to the cafetorium, amazed at the difference in energy from regular school days. The darkness and silence of the normally chaotic hallways were peaceful and unsettling. A place that is usually so active seems like a purgatory portal when it's not buzzing.

I checked my phone. He'd read the message but had yet to respond. That wasn't like him and now I worried. Had some Saint Ignatius meat head cornered him somewhere and fucked him up good? Where no one could hear his screams, the incessant crying. Was he lying beaten and bloodied in some obscure campus corner? Begging for my help while I stared into the lit void of my phone like a clueless moth?

The light in Lightfoot's classroom was on and the door ajar. I heard whispering as I brought my fist up to knock. Sounds of intimacy within stopped me. Their hushed, whispered tones matched our night-time conversations that ended with us lying atop one another, bunched up like exhausted kittens.

"You better use that number during winter break," Lightfoot said.

"Of course."

"And make sure to watch *It's a Wonderful Life*. Can't believe a supposedly avid film student like you has never seen it."

I peeked in just enough. They were at a corner of the room they thought hid them from view.

"Check to both," Amaury said, using his index finger like a pen in the air. "I really have to get back. Bailey's texted me like crazy and I swear to God if anyone fucks with her, I'll make the news tonight."

"I love what you two have going."

"She's my girl," Amaury said.

I smiled, swallowing back the gasp threatening to leap from my throat.

"Okay, I'm off. Give me a kiss to sustain me through our time apart," Amaury said.

To this day, I don't know why the fuck. But I held up my phone and recorded as Amaury's and Lightfoot's lips joined, tongues coiling on and around one another. Holy shit. That's how fucking charming Amaury was.

I coached myself on the way back to the cafetorium. Act as normal. Nothing happened. When Amaury returned, I was back at my post by the snacks. "Dude? What the fuck?" I threw my hands in the air for effect.

"I know, I know, but. . ." He looked around to make sure no one was listening. "Please don't make me tell you what happened in that bathroom. So embarrassing."

Well played. I didn't push it. It was his secret to share whenever he was ready. To Lightfoot's credit and my heaving heart, I'd never seen him so happy. He danced with a Brazilian intensity I'd only seen in films. He was grabbing me and grinding up so close, Principal Serna warned us a couple of times, then threatened three-day suspension after the third.

Amaury leaned in to whisper. "Their closed minds are not ready for what we're about to give them."

As the night went on, Amaury pulled me in to his dampening chest, his sweat landing on my forehead. I didn't care at all. I wanted to open my mouth and gulp it all down. Our body heat locked us into a humid bubble where just two of us existed. I figured he was fantasizing about Lightfoot. But I didn't care. I was getting my fantasy. I had an open mind.

That night was the most physical I'd ever get with Amaury

Sambrano, the center of my seventeen-year-old life. So, dance on, and let him do what he wanted, let him play it out in his mind however he needed to keep moving into me like that. I loved what was happening and did not want it to stop. Stares, administrative threats, and narrow-minded opinions be damned.

We cleared the dance floor and lit it up until the last song.

Amaury walked me home. A static tingle of energy hissed in my stomach and radiated down into my pussy. No one, before or since, has ever made me feel so uncontrollably hot.

Back home, a cold shower felt good but did nothing to tamp me. In the pitch darkness of my room, I curled under the blanket, pulled out the phone, cued the video, and rubbed myself silly until pulling back soaking fingers, reining up quivering legs.

The satisfaction I felt with—having attended a second high school dance with the hottest boy in school; being twenty pounds lighter; seeing a lot more boys checking me out as their jealous dates rolled eyes; having a best friend with whom I shared a crazy secret only a true friendship could keep locked down tight—was enough to rub another one out.

I slept like a goddam newborn that night.

———

Three nights later on Christmas Eve, Amaury came clean. We were at his house. I finally had some place to be 'twas the night before Christmas.

The beauty? Eliana Sambrano was an early sleeper. Soon as she was out, we had a run of the place and her ample wine cellar. Outside on the back deck overlooking the lake, we're half a bottle down and I am floating. Hands numbed, fingertips tingling in pin pricks that made everything I touched feel like the vibration between my legs during what were now nightly rubbing sessions. I made good use of that video and my very vivid, imaginative knack for sexual fantasy.

I wanted to hug the entire world. Because Amaury was my world. I was all over him, because what did it matter? Being an attention whore, he was loving it.

Amaury poured us each a glass, evenly measuring out until the bottle emptied.

"No more?" I said, pouting.

"There's more. Don't worry. We'll be here all night. Bailey, there's something I want to tell you." His tone serious.

Fail-safe point. I let him talk, making sure not to overdo my reactions one way or the other, lest he felt judged or suspect I already knew.

Looking up at the night sky as if sketching Lightfoot in constellation, he verbalized his love, said he was smitten and had found his soulmate. "Who would've known Prince Charming taught film in a Florida Catholic school?"

"So. You really think I'm the devil now?" he asked, downing the rest of his glass.

I downed mine and instantly knew it was a bad call based on my unseasoned liver.

"I know."

His eyebrows furrowed together. "What?"

"I know. I went to the bathroom at the dance and saw both of you kissing in the classroom like a couple of freshmen."

"Bitch." This wasn't said the same way as thousand times before. He was actually calling me a bitch. He stood in the same posture he used with the queen bees. Then, the smile across his face was an immediate warm blanket. "Why didn't you tell me anything?"

Thank Christ. "Because it isn't my secret to tell. We're going to need another bottle for this shit."

He hugged me tight. "That's why I love you so much, Bailey Cohen. You know how to be a true friend. Let's toast." He scrambled into the house and came back with a bottle tucked under his arm. We toasted to our friendship. Then, he grabbed my hand and swore me to secrecy.

"Of course."

"No, seriously. You can't tell anyone because this is a grown man we're talking about, a professional. If anyone finds out about this, I lose the love of my life and he loses his career. We're both done for."

To seal the pact, to really let me know this wasn't just your run of the mill, we smoked pot together, secret, he kissed me. Not a pop, either. It was the longest, hardest kiss I'd ever get from him. The one kiss, amongst all my guy kisses, I have never forgotten. Had I been standing outside the frame of that kiss, like at Lightfoot's door, I'd have seen the night sky open, sparks fly, shooting stars descend. Every pleasure point in and outside my body writhe from intense pressure. A unicorn had landed in my lap. This would not happen again. I grabbed the back of his head and pressed our mouths in tight to ensure a few more seconds of the best moment of my life.

Amaury never pulled away. "I didn't know you could be that intense," he said when it was over.

"You have no idea how you've changed my life."

"I love you too. We're going to be together forever. Where you go, I go. Ride or die."

"Just promise you'll be careful, okay?" I said.

Amaury blushed for the first time in our history and raised his right hand in scout's honor.

"And, I swear to God, if he hurts you, I'm hanging him upside down by the flagpole," I said.

"I promise I'll help you tighten the rope."

It was the type of Christmas I'd always dreamed of sharing whenever I dreamed up what it would be like to have a true friend.

Our families even gathered for breakfast one morning.

Eliana Sambrano could sit in any setting and charm the pants off the room. It was clear where Amaury got his spunk and flamboyance.

Amaury and Lightfoot constantly messaged one another and every day he seemed to fall a little bit more in love, gushing how he couldn't wait until graduation and whisk away with his older beau to an open-minded European country where they could both be together without societal taboos dangling over their heads like impending nooses.

The best I could do for myself was live vicariously through this Nabokovesque relationship. Pretending it was me he gushed over. That we would set off to Europe in the summer, to make love on an isolated beach, drinking bottle after bottle of local wine.

————

After break and back in school, everyone else was miserable to return and only offered us, the happiest misfits on campus, hate-fuck looks as we paraded hand in hand through the halls with Grand Canyon-wide smiles.

Leeza Cifuentes as we passed with her girls in tow: "Why the fuck are you two so happy?"

"Because neither of us made the terrible decision of pairing that eyeliner with that shirt, sweetie," Amaury said without pause.

Arianna Viasco giggled.

Leeza pounced on her. "Are you fucking serious right now?"

Amaury smiled and winked at me.

Leeza and Johanna stormed off with Arianna doggedly chasing after.

"Ah, how easy to drive a wedge between the vapid and stupid." Amaury was thrilled with his work.

Classes were great, the curriculum was easy, and Lightfoot and Amaury couldn't have been any cuter. The romantic tension was so obvious, I was glad it was only three people in the room. Lightfoot didn't seem to be trying to suppress it.

At lunch, he wouldn't stop talking about how cute Lightfoot looked, wondering whether he'd dressed up special just for him. Saying he needed to start upping his own game.

"I love what you have going," I said. "But maybe you should try and be a little less obvious. Bring it down a notch."

"I'm being subtle. You want me like this?" He put his hands together in prayer mode.

"I'm just saying, it was pretty out there in class today. I wouldn't want anyone to find out and there goes your happiness."

"You're blowing this out of proportion."

"I think you're not listening to me," I said.

"And I think maybe you should mind your own business." He stood and walked off with more than five minutes before next period.

Leeza had been watching it all from the cafetorium door. She came straight at me and said as she passed. "Trouble in paradise?"

"Fuck off," I yelled after her.

Fuck focusing the rest of the day. Between figuring from where the argument stemmed, and what I could have done differently, voices, lessons, and time, were a blur. How long would this last? How long before me and Amaury were talking again? My day was completely different without him.

Mister Yu droning on and on about motifs in *The Great Gatsby* was like sandpaper being slowly, perpetually, rubbed together.

I had to cut out, shift my thinking. The girls' bathroom behind the quad was always empty, so I settled there, inside the last stall. Where I propped my foot on the toilet, cued the video, and went to town. Didn't take long before my legs shook, fingers glistened, and my head swam in post-cum ether. I breathed in deep and smiled as satisfaction pushed away anxiety.

With a glass-eyed, dreamy stare, I rode out the rest of Yu's faulty lecture, following the clock's second-hand trajectory toward 2:30. Thinking, man, how good I'd gotten with my fingers. Thinking, shit, this beef with Amaury is ridiculous and pointless. Right after class, I'll send the first smoke signal and hope this beef would end with us walking home together.

My phone wasn't in my pocket or bag. What the fuck? Shit. Must have left it on the sink when grabbing paper towels to dry my hands. In my loopy, post-cum, satiated state, I completely spaced.

My hand stabbed the air.

"Yes, Miss Cohen?"

"I need to step out."

"Nope. You already used your one break."

"But, I really—"

"Want afterschool detention? Because that's what's happening if you keep interrupting my lecture."

Mister Fucking Yu. The class idiots ohhhed and ahhhed like the sheep they were following one another's social cues.

Soon as the bell clanged, I bolted across campus to the back of the quad, not giving three shits about bumping students who cursed under their breaths.

Leeza Cifuentes came my way from the direction of the bathroom. Shit-eating grin widening her face. Had a right mind to ram into her.

Then, Queen Bee held up the phone. "Lose something?"

I panted out insincere "thanks" and yanked it from her clutch.

How long did this bitch have it and why hadn't I programmed a lock screen? God damn it!

As expected, Amaury wasn't there to walk me home. Petrified, I didn't send that smoke signal just yet, the whole way home convincing myself even heartless bitches like Leeza Cifuentes had moral limits.

That afternoon, I replaced the exercise routine with a bowl of ice cream. When mom came knocking, wondering about Amaury, I snapped. She faced the funk of all the shit that had gone on that day, which was unfair because she had no way of knowing. Such are things in a seventeen-year-old world.

"Okay," Mom said, lowering her voice like she did when she was controlling the impulse to scream at me. "I'm here if you need to talk."

Fuck yes I needed to talk, but the only person who could provide that solace, my shaman with the perfect spell, was mad at me. If things continued on their track, he might soon excommunicate me all together.

Almost two hours later, after not answering her at all, Mom just barged in.

"Mom! What the fuck?"

Everyone had limits. I'd get smacked for that. But, no.

"Have you heard from Amaury?" she asked.

"No."

"Did you know this was going on?" Mom turned her phone screen to me.

Across a Saint Ignatius parent text-message thread I had no idea about, was splashed my screen capture of Amaury and Lightfoot's intimate moment. That titillating image was now a billboard screaming back at me: *IDIOT, SHITTY FRIEND, PERVERT, FAILURE. YOU'RE DONE, BITCH!*

By nightfall, it had found its way onto Saint Ignatius students', parents', and administrators' phones.

––––––––––

Mom's voice was a droning hum, worse than Yu's, the worst I've ever heard. "That disgusting image is all over the place. Parents and students are ping-ponging it. Do you have this teacher?"

The Empire State Building perched on my chest, my toes tingled. There wasn't enough oxygen in the room, let alone the house. I had to get the fuck out and bolted through the front door without thinking. Mom's screams filled the neighborhood behind me. They said I'd better come back, or I was in serious trouble.

Eliana Sambrano actually answered the door. One look on her usually glamorous face and I knew that image had T-boned its way into the house. Sporting eyeliner-smeared cheeks, she clutched a half-empty glass of wine in one hand, a smoldering cigarette in the other. "What? You want in? You want to come in and see meu filho pagão."

She turned, stumbling clumsily. Was she blocking my entrance or clearing a path?

When she finally stepped aside, Amaury rushed out and grabbed a mound of my hair, yanking to tear away scalp. I was outside again, rolling in dirt he kicked all over me, in my eyes and mouth.

The inside of the house filled with Miss Sambrano's screams. Something in Portuguese about the devil in jeans.

Amaury kept kicking up dirt. "Choke on it, you dumb cunt. I'm never going to forgive you for this. You don't deserve any happiness. Get the fuck out of my life and stay there. You're dead as far as I'm concerned. Boceta traiçoeira, venenosa."

I bawled, all the whole way home.

God bless her, Mom had a cup of coffee ready the next morning. No one said good morning or asked how the other was. "Teacher's been arrested," she said. "Maybe you should stay home."

Saint Ignatius was Bedlam. Cops and reporters cramped its perimeter. School security checked everyone's bags as we walked in. It took almost an hour under the hot, sticky Florida morning sun before we were inside. Principal Serna and other administrators directed us to the gym for a special assembly.

In as long as I could remember, no one fucked with me. They stared hard, sure, but it was as if they didn't know what to make of the girl caught right in the middle of this, the school and town's most scandalous, sordid cluster fuck. Would I apologize? Hang myself? Leave town to never be heard from again? What would I do? The girl whose masturbatory inspiration sparked a controversy no one in this school, or town, was strapped in for.

The gym buzzed like a bug zapper with rumor and speculation. People killed their hushed conversations as I passed. This was Salem, and my evil stare could kill cattle. I sat as far back, and high up, as the stacked bleachers would allow. My back flat against the gym's concrete wall.

I looked down at my incriminating phone, the video long deleted. Amaury had not reached out and I didn't dare call or send a message.

A shadow suddenly loomed. Arianna Viasco stood over me like a post.

"What?" I snapped.

She was on the verge of tears. "I just want to ask how you're doing."

Boo fucking hoo. I stood and yelled right in her entitled, deceptive face. "Fuck off!"

Everyone. Everyone in that gym turned toward us. Some snickered, others bumped elbows and pointed.

Arianna ran out in tears.

Principal Serna bumped the microphone against his forearm. "All right. That's enough. Bailey Cohen, in my office as soon as this assembly is over."

Students ohhed, ahhed, and whistled.

"Want me to start slinging out detentions left and right? Keep it up," Serna yelled. That shut them up fast. Serna paced back and forth looking at his shoes; left, right, left. "Ladies and gentlemen, many of you are well aware of what's going on and we want to assure you this campus is safe and always has your best interest in mind."

Someone sucked their teeth.

Serna scanned the bleachers, breathing heavy into the microphone. The dragon was woken. "By the end of the day, we will send a letter to your parents explaining the situation as best we can given the legal limitations we're under at this time, which change moment to moment."

Someone in a sharp suit walked over to Serna and whispered.

The principal nodded. "Yes, thank you. Having said that, you see there are a lot of reporters waiting around, please do not speak to any of them. Just try to go about your day as routinely as possible, considering the circumstances. Thank you. Are there any questions?" The last part came out in a sigh of exhaustion.

Teenaged hands pierced the air.

"That don't involve the situation."

All but two lowered.

Serna pointed to Arianna Viasco at the other side of the gym.

"Are we going to all of our classes today? Because I heard there might be early dismissal."

A buzz of excitement snaked through the bleachers.

"All right, everyone. Calm down. As of right now, this is a regular day of school, which means you'll be attending all classes."

The excitement went from buzz to collective groan.

Serna fought for volume and control. "Anyone who leaves early will be considered absent. Anyone caught skipping will be dealt with as any other day. That you can count on." He checked his watch. "All right, ladies and gentlemen. We've got just a couple of minutes before the end of first period, so we'll ride it out in here until the bell. We ask second-period teachers to take morning attendance. Oh, Cohen, don't forget. My office."

More ohhs and ahhs.

"Shut up!" Serna shouted.

———

Principal Serna was on the phone when I knocked. He waved me in, still finishing his conversation. "There's nothing for me to say right now and we won't be releasing a statement until the district conducts its own investigation. . . No, no. My answer isn't going to change. . . Fine. Call the school board all you like. They're going to give you roughly the same answer. You have a great day too." He slammed the phone and muttered, "Asshole." Then realized what he'd done. "Jesus, I'm sorry. This is not a normal situation here. Sit."

Serna leaned back and joined his fingertips in a triangle propping up his chin. "Bailey Cohen. Good friends with Amaury Sambrano. Correct?"

Shit.

I nodded.

Serna leaned toward a yellow memo pad scribbled with notes in crazy chicken scratch. "We need to be abundantly clear that everything you're going to tell me is the absolute truth. Understand?"

"Yes, sir."

"What's with this picture floating around?"

"I didn't send it out."

"I didn't say you did. I'm asking what's with it?"

"It's a screen capture of a video I recorded."

"Good. Now we're getting somewhere."

"When did you take this picture?"

"Couple weeks back."

"Be more specific."

"At Winter Formal."

Serna wrote WINTER FORMAL and made a big production of underling it with three slashes that cut the office's silence. "They ask you to record this video?"

"Of course not. What sense does that make?"

"I'm just asking. So. You take this picture, and they have no clue."

"None."

"And this is the first you find out about its floating around?"

"Yup."

"You said you'd be honest with me, Cohen."

I covered my heart with my right palm. "Swear to God."

"All right. No need for theatrics. It was only two of you in that film class. You never witnessed anything untoward between Misters Sambrano and Lightfoot?"

"Nothing."

"No flirting? Solicitations for Amaury to stay after class alone? Preferential treatment?"

"How can there be preferential treatment with just two students in class?"

"Let's stay on topic. Yes or no?"

"No, sir."

"Were you aware they were communicating privately outside of school?"

"No."

"What was the picture for?"

"Video."

"Fine. The video. What were you keeping the video for, Bailey?"

Fuck him. I didn't budge.

Serna furiously scribbled as he spoke. "I have lots to do, but this isn't over by a sight, Ms. Cohen. You're still on my hook. This thing is just starting, and we'll be seeing each other again very soon. You can set your watch to that shit."

He didn't apologize this time.

"Want to write that down too?" I asked.

"I suggest you shut your trap and split before I decide to really start digging," he said without looking up.

By the time the grilling was over, it was third period. Thankfully. Brother Martin's World Religions class was about as exciting as watching paint dry. The octogenarian lectured and lectured through bubble gum snaps, distant snores, and cellphone dings. I could easily sleep through and wake up fifty minutes closer to dismissal.

Mom was right. I should have just stayed home.

Arianna Viasco was halfway up the hall when I rounded the corner toward the religion building.

I'd been a bitch to her, the kind she'd be to someone else. Maybe it was time to make things right. "Hey, I'm sorry about this morning. I'm just. . ." I started.

"No, I get it. I haven't been the nicest person to you. I want to say sorry too."

"You haven't been the worst either."

"Leeza went too far with this. I get she's trying to be the queen of mean, but this is too much," Arianna said.

"Where is she?"

Arianna shrugged. "Don't know and don't care."

"Hey, listen. If you happen to—" I started.

Destiny meant that statement never to finish. A line of students ran through the halls in the direction of the quad, pulling me with them. Teachers and students spilled out of classrooms. Someone yelled at the others to look up, at the jumper.

A massive crowd filled the quad next to the cafetorium. I squeezed between bodies, past pointy elbows, around plaid skirts and fitted chinos. Body heat and tension thick in the crowd. Midway to the front, Arianna latched on to one of my belt loops until our dysfunctional two-car train made it to just a couple of rows from the front where school security and administration formed a human wall. As if they could block what was happening high above across the street.

"I need all hands on deck right now. We have a serious

situation," Yuset, the head of security, yelled frantically into her radio. I'd never seen the big oaf of a woman so frazzled.

There was my boy Amaury Sambrano. Perched at the edge of the office building across the street, pacing back and forth on its ledge, screaming at the cops below, who desperately tried talking him down. Whatever he shouted was inaudible. People on my side yelled for him to come down like he could hear. As if he would listen.

It would be like that faggot to do something so goddam over the top. To commit to going up that high as his own way of saying, *HEY, EVERYONE. LOOK AT ME. OVER HERE.*

"Get down," Ariana yelled.

"He can't hear you," I said but she didn't hear me.

Amaury yelled. To this day, I couldn't tell you what it was. In the moment though, concretely, and with all confidence, I understood it was the last time I'd ever see Amaury Sambrano in the flesh. So, I forced myself to stare at every single one of his movements and actions. Goddam, he's so beautiful. With a sense of his own I'd never known before and would not find after. Even in this, his most desperate, final, vulnerable, moment, Amaury Sambrano was less person than occurrence.

Turning away would have been the ultimate betrayal of the only person I'd ever been able to call, or consider, a friend. In the unlikely event Amaury spotted me in the crowd, I wanted to be sure he saw me staring right back at, and through, him. Into his beating, anxious heart.

Amaury shouted something again.

"Will everyone just shut the fuck up?" I yelled. Swear to God to this day, the crowd went quiet.

Then Amaury pointed. Swear to God to this day, right at

me. The cop on the ground, with a megaphone, pleaded for him to come down.

Serna barreled through the crowd toward his security team at the school's back fence, the closest they could get before the police cordon.

Arianna bumped me. "You think he'll do it?"

"He's up there and he's high as shit." What a line when your best friend is stories up about to end his life.

Then a collective gasp as Amaury dove and spiked to the ground. Swear to God to this day, I heard the thud. Arianna swore later his body bounced on impact.

Arianna was the first to scream? That gave way to hysterics that tore like wildfire through the panicked crowd.

Yuset turned away, shutting her eyes from the horrid image.

"Everybody into the gymnasium now!" Serna yelled.

Panic ensued as people hollered, cried; some threw up.

Serna yelled into the megaphone, "Everybody seek shelter in the gymnasium. Right! Now!"

It was like herding cats. Some scrambled toward Amaury, others away. Swear to God to this day, some took pictures and video of Amaury Sambrano sending himself to his crypt.

Police rushed to cover Amaury's distended body amid a cacophony of verbal commands, walkie-talkies squawking, emergency sirens filling the air.

"Let's go," Arianna said, yanking me in an unknown direction.

No idea where the fuck I was being pulled, my world was rudderless. There was no order, no joy, no point to any of it. No one, let alone your girl, was in control.

I pulled from Arianna's grip and ran full speed until my lungs couldn't take in any more air and my legs were concrete. I ran inside the gym, hauled ass back up the last row of bleachers to the same spot against the concrete wall as that morning, curled into a ball, and went to sleep. Convinced my heart would explode and I'd never come to.

Came to later that night, inside my bedroom, all alone. I turned on the TV.

Local and national news affiliates were camped outside the Saint Ignatius perimeter; now the spot of an Amaury memorial. On camera extolling were some of the same people who relentlessly called him a fag, tugged at his clothes, mocked his fabulous walk, told me at lunch to "save some pizza for the rest of us." Now they cried for the cameras, laid flowers for close-ups, went on and on about how it just wasn't fair he was gone. "Such a positive light burnt out much too quickly," someone said. To this day, I couldn't tell you who it was.

It fucking lit me like tinder.

Can you believe these bandwagoning cunts? I heard Amaury, clear as a bell. That fabulous voice forever stripped from the soundtrack of my life.

Then, my best friend's voice was drowned out by another voice.

One actually there, on camera. Leeza Cifuentes. Holding up a makeshift poster with cardboard cut-out letters: **NEVER FORGET AMAURY SAMBRANO. WE MISS YOU FOREVER!**

"I can't believe he's gone," she said, then cracked a smile. "Yeah, he was different. God knows he was flashy." She giggled. "But he was a light in this school and today that light was. . ." Too overcome with emotion to finish, she buried her head in Johanna Carrascal's chest. The camera held on her sobbing.

I beelined, pile drove, my way to the memorial. Know

those revenge flicks where the good guy finally figures out the culprit's actually his best friend who's been helping him the whole time? That it was the guy helping him solve the mystery who was responsible for the entire journey to begin with? That walk they have during the final act? When they're going to burn their house down and everything, one, they love? Put two slugs in their head.

That was your girl then. Such a bad-ass walk it was, the crowd opened a path for me right toward Leeza, who'd claimed another news camera for herself. "Oh my God. This is Amaury's best friend, Bailey," Leeza said.

On live TV, ladies and gentlemen. Don't believe me, find it on the net. I first ripped the poster from Leeza's hand. Then, invoking Amaury, grabbed the queen bitch's ponytail and flung her to the floor, tearing some hair out. On local and national news affiliates, I kicked that bitch in the ribs like Jet Li in *Ip Man*. Not done, I straddled Leeza's chest and pummeled her face until my knuckles went bloody. Her beautiful, privileged, prom-queen face tenderized, softened, and broke.

Then, swear to God, I leaned into the bitch to bite the nose off her face before someone scooped me up.

Next thing I knew, I was inside a cop car en route to processing.

Saint Ignatius expelled your girl.

After therapy and some legal loop de loop, graduation— from J.R.E. Lee Educational Center (opportunity school)—came one year later than planned.

The University of Florida loved my college essay's up-by-the-bootstraps story. No scholarship, though. Schools are reticent handing scholarships to a certified fucking loca.

The physical therapy track was easy as Lexapro, which tampered down your girl's grit, brought the pride down a peg, and made me just complacent and quiet enough to complete my bachelor's.

———————

Bailey Cohen learned to retract her claws, loosen her shoulders, and relax.

Like, for example, that time mom and dad came at her about how she needed to get her shit together, quit living in an efficiency next door to a reservation. Or later, when live-in boyfriend Gabe Acevedo had something to say about almost everything dealing with the way she ran her life.

Got to be, I didn't need medication.

Fine. In all honesty, booze replaced the anti-depressants.

What do people want? The therapist said life is a series of baby steps. A marathon, not a sprint.

The grit bottled up until I was complacent taking up residence in a Miami Beach high rise with a boyfriend described by her therapist as verbally and emotionally abusive.

Why make waves?

Then, Sandy Mangual comes crashing down onto Collins Avenue in a shower of glass, blood, and screams.

And who was there, front row center, to profit from the spotlight and proximity? A boyfriend who some have described as a psychopath with a camera and social media platform.

Let's see that grit, girl. Sandblast the motherfucker.

Clear as a campana, I hear Amaury Sambrano. I hear my best friend again.

Se muy bien porque

the Manguals nos pidieron este tipo de "favor". Somos misfits.

Especialmente este tipo right here. Con poco más de cuarenta sobre el lomo, que carajo tengo to show for it? No house, no car, no job, no country. Un gitano wandering the Earth. Like. . . ¿Como se llamaba el show Americano con el chino que no era chino? Kung Fu! That's who I am. El tipo from Kung Fu. ¿La gran diferencia? I'm not going around helping people or making a difference. So far, lo único que he hecho en estos Estados Unidos is try to blend in and disappear.

As immigrants like me are expected to in cities like Miami. Work, exist, be grateful at having the opportunity to live en una ciudad with such big beautiful buildings and cars big as tanks barreling through the widest roads I've ever known. Open the tap; agua limpia, fria, y gratis. No reason for anyone to die of thirst en estos Estados Unidos. Be grateful for the wage given under the table because immigrants are off the books and if the government catches us being paid por debajo la mesa, Adios, pipo. Ese Tio Sam es un hijo de puta en cuanto cobrando lo que se le debe.

So, shhhh. Calladito. Don't ask too many questions, keep

any complaints aqui en medio de la garganta. Remember, it's a system. None is perfect. Every system needs oil and fuel lubricating the motor. Pistons that keep it churning.

Yo y los parecidos a mi, so many names for them—ilegales, clandestinos, aliens—are the belts grinding away, keeping the motor going day in and day out, fast and hard. The belts in a motor can't break, must run consistently. Anda, sigue, empuja sin parar. The motor keeps turning until the system operates without fail. Why check under the hood when the motor's purring so smoothly?

Hasta que se rompe, destrozado de tanto output day in and day out. That's when the belt gets noticed. Cuando para de trabajar, exhausted from long hours not logged on a time sheet. Cansado de eyes rolling when you ask someone to please repeat because, "My English not so good."

Me duelen las orejas de oír, "In this country…"

In this country, trabajo doce horas al dia to live in a small efficiency at the back of a single-family home on the border between Little Havana and Miami. Y nunca he sido comemierda. Se muy bien que with all the construction happening in the area, I'll have to leave there, too. A lo mejor I find a construction job nearby. Construction here supposedly pays really good, pero my back and legs aren't what they used to be. Y sin seguro de salud. . . olvidalo.

Siempre hablan en Cuba de The American Dream. House, car, family, kids, steady work. Houses are demasiado expensive. I tried going to the bank to open an account. Pero, sin papeles, olvidalo. Casi ni tengo tiempo de desayunar before it's off to work again. A ese paso, I'll never afford a place even half like the Manguals. The American Dream se agotó hace tiempo.

I stare out the window at Las Brisas, my universe the last two years. I was a good slave. Quedandome callado, covering for the documented workers too sick or emborrachados to come into work. Tranquilo, que el reliable guajirito de Castillo will cover your shift.

Y pa que? For Gabe Acevedo to come in and take it all because he didn't feel safe. For David Schecter to forget two years of hard work en un chasquear de dedos because money is thicker than loyalty.

On the Collins skyline, high rises jut up into the sky. At the western half of the island, casas que mas nunca pudiera pagar. Miami Beach exists because The American Dream is real, but it's not casa, carro, y familia. It's about cutting corners. La ley del menor esfuerzo. Getting ahead by being the foot pressing the accelerator, grinding it down to the floor. The motor runs at full, chaotic speed, churning, grinding. The belts whirl frantically like a hamster wheel, pistons pump, oil and fuel course through. Until there's no way to keep up such a frenetic pace. The engine gives out en un grito final de humo y chispas. The foot steps off the accelerator, gives the motor a friendly pat on the back, and abandons it, oxidado, enraizado, olvidado.

"Yo le dije que no comprará un apartamento tan caro." Tomas Mangual intersects my daydream gaze across Miami. "Y pa que? A million-dollar price tag, God knows how much in association fees y mira." He points his coffee mug, with whiskey inside, at the balcony, where the railing is bent toward the street and shattered glass twinkles in the moonlight. "Shoddy construction." Tomas takes a sip and asks if I want some.

¿Porque no? Este es el sueño. Standing next to the man I've only ever seen on the front pages of newspapers or magazines. The Puerto Rican development mogul who's worked to put his island on the map, keep his industry churning with Puerto Ricans, by Puerto Ricans. Eight-hour work days, the best healthcare coverage, stock in the company, a union that protects them as the company expands its reach across Latin America and the U.S.

Tomas sniffles.

Por respeto, no miro al padre de luto.

"No se que hacer, Bernardo. This pain inside me gets bigger and bigger every second. I don't hear people when they talk. I don't hear myself. Everything doesn't make sense. None of it. I don't know if I make sense."

Se muy bien que nothing making sense makes complete sense. "Hace años perdí a la persona más importante de mi vida."

"¿Que hiciste?"

"Me desapareci, aquí a los Estados Unidos." There's no point trying to inspire someone with stock phrases. *God's plan. Some day this will all make sense. Heaven has another angel.* Pa' la pinga con palabras inspiradas cuando las orejas lo que quieren es que el mundo se callé.

"Maybe I need to disappear too," Tomas whispers.

"What's so secretive?" Ximena Mangual grabs a glass from the pantry. Her smile fades when I turn to her pero Tomas se queda congelado, still crying. "Gabe is picking up Janaina and she said he doesn't sound mad anymore."

Bailey comes into the kitchen smiling, leaning against the counter, signaling Ximena for una taza like a longtime roommate. "Of course he wouldn't. He's so fucking predictable, that guy. If there's one thing you can set your watch to, it's that Gabe Acevedo will follow pussy right off a ledge."

Tomas and Ximena turn to her.

Silence engulfs the room.

"Oh my God. I swear I didn't mean. . ."

"Shhh. Dejalo asi," Ximena says, passing her a glass.

Miro al piso and shake my head. La quiero muchísimo pero a veces Bailey dice cosas que se pasan.

"Bueno," Jimena says. "Now that we all have glasses, un brindis. Here's to the plan, here's to vengeance, the memory of my son, and how good it feels, however good we can feel anymore, that Gabe Acevedo is no more."

"Lo vamos a descojonar todo," I say porque tengo que decir algo.

Tomas chuckles. "Asi mismo. This motherfucker needs to pay."

Tomamos el whiskey, all the way through. Nos miramos uno a otro. El plan se materializado. It exists. Esta es la parte mas difícil: committing. Doing instead of talking. Engine roaring como el apocalypto, pedal to the metal, el carro flying to wherever it's steered, even if it means mangled full speed into a wall.

Ximena pours again and we all drink, again. Committed.

All of us going all the way. Intimidad stronger than beauty, sex, love, the heart. La venganza hecha corporeal, nacida high above Collins Avenue, ready to be released into the world. For Gabe Acevedo to absorb.

It feels good doing bad.

Tears, heartache, sleepless nights, embitterment with God, obsessively planning everything down to the last detail. All come down to this.

Once this is over, Ximena Mangual disappears from the real world we know, the illusion of what the real world is and begins existing as Sandy Mangual's mom until I die. I'm an actress. Whatever works, I can do. Here, tonight, is the end of the small-time telenovela actress gracing so many covers of Spanish-language magazines. I'm grateful for the opportunity and the massive amounts of positive energy it fostered. Pero, como dice Marc Anthony, *Todo a su Tiempo*. Taking things any farther than they need be is, plain and simply, greedy and tragic.

If it wasn't because I was so tired, I'd move on to directing. I was always better at giving orders than taking them. Por esa precisa razón fue que se fue Tomas. But that's another story for another time. I'll have plenty of time to tell it once this is over.

Janaina looks beautiful. Her dress leaves nothing to the imagination except that her two beautiful, perky melons might spill out any moment. Tits and teeth, like she likes to say, pero tonight she's not saying much. Says she's nervous and repulsed. Doesn't want to get any closer to Gabe but tonight's the night she really has to get him comfortable and confident so the quintet can step in. Everyone's at their marks, ready to spring into action. Janaina sips a glass of champagne as we run through the plan.

The hired town car takes Janaina to Gabe's. She'll spin a story that the editors want to make good on their word. This car is just a small symbol of what's to come of the collaboration. Janaina's going to sell the sexuality, making sure to sit just right, flash some teeth and tits, build up what's to come after dinner. Logic will veer from Gabe's head to the rock-hard cock that will lead him wherever she says. De verdad que los hombres son del carajo.

Midway through the second, third glass of champagne, she'll pull out a little pill from between her titties and tell Gabe it's ecstasy, to take the edge off. She'll tell him not to worry, he won't start peaking until after the meeting. When they'll go right back to his place and celebrate their new collaboration with more collaboration.

It's dark when the town car arrives at Bernardo's efficiency. The set is prepped for filming. Tomas and Bernardo hide behind a hedgerow separating the efficiency from Calle Ocho. Ximena and Tomas are inside waiting with Elias, who works at Mount Sinai, was threatened into Gabe's picture-taking scheme, and can't stand the son of a bitch despite being a self-professed pacifist. Librame de las aguas mansas que de las malas me libro yo.

For one night's work—serious work—they're paying him enough to comfortably follow Phish around this and next summer. And a little more than a year's salary at Mount Sinai. Just to help scrub the conscience clear.

El pobre. First thing he asked, "I have to kill anyone?"

"Not quite, just silence them," Tomas said.

When the car pulls up, Janaina's out first. It's clear Gabe's taken the pill, which was not ecstasy but is actually Ketamine. She helps Gabe maintain balance but he's still lucid enough to slur out that, "this place doesn't look like an office." As he pulls his hand away from Janaina's, Tomas and Bernardo rush from behind the bushes. Tomas throws the sack over his head and Bernardo lifts him on to his shoulder like in an old war movie.

Inside, me and Bailey make quick work of hog-tying him—like we practiced five too many times, according to everyone—face-down on to the bed.

Gabe puts up a slow fight as the Ketamine strangles his faculties.

The timing is working out just as anticipated.

Bryan injects him with a general anesthetic that, coupled with the Ketamine, gives him the time he needs to get his serious work done.

The entire efficiency is covered wall to wall, floor to ceiling, with plastic sheeting. It rustles beneath our feet as we five step back to watch Bryan perform.

Madre de Dios is he good. So good, I wonder aloud why he isn't a surgeon.

"Working on it but med school's expensive as hell and not all of us are blessed with a silver spoon like this prick. I can only take so many credits a semester while working full-time."

Tomas, who has not had a drink the entire day because "quiero saborear cada segundo de esto," tells Bryan when all this is done, he'll throw in the money to cover the rest of his full-time track, as long as he promises to completely focus on studies and graduate as soon as possible.

"You realize how much money that is, sir?"

"Yeah. But, look at you, you're a fucking sculptor."

"The world could use more people like you," Bryan says as he snaps on the surgical saw and brings it down on the metacarpophalangeal joint crease, cutting a perfect three-sixty loop, severing Gabe's left thumb like butter.

The boy's an artist, deftly tamping the wound with a towel as he picks up the cauterizer and welds the hole with the grace of a ballerina, the confidence of an orchestra composer who knows when every note should drop and exactly how it should sound.

Mesmerized, we five hypnotically watch as he severs the right thumb.

"All right. Can you guys flip him over? Gently as possible, please."

Bernardo and Tomas make swift work of it.

"This is going to be messier," Bryan warns, grabbing forceps. "I'm going to need some help."

We hesitate, ping-ponging stares back and forth in a visual Mexican standoff.

"Fuck it," Bailey says, stepping forward.

"Excellent. Thanks so much. I'm going to open his mouth." He hands her the forceps. "You take these, clamp down just past the tip of his tongue and pull toward you. Hold it there for me steady as you can, okay? I promise to make it as quick as possible."

Gabe's tongue jutting out, Bryan lays it between a pair of large surgical shears. In one, two, three pumps, it too is untethered.

"Now, hold his mouth open for me," he tells Bailey urgently.

In minutes, Gabe's tongue is cauterized. Bryan turns the thumbless mute on his side. Time for disposal.

We arrive at the quiet spot behind an abandoned marine textile factory on the Miami river. Gabe still unconscious, we wrap him tight inside an old blanket and leave him face up.

We leave the bottle of ketamine inside his right pocket. Lo va a necesitar. In his left, his phone's memo pad app announces in large bold letters: **MY NAME IS GABRIEL ACEVEDO. I'VE DONE SOME BAD SHIT**. Thumbing through the phone, whoever discovers him will find pictures of Sandy's body, transactions and threatening messages to Pablo Porras at *O, Respinga*, surveillance footage of his beating at the hands of Bernardo Castillo. Janaina Brilhante inside his home, recorded without her knowledge, home-shot footage of his masturbatory habits.

When Gabe Acevedo comes to, he'll find he has to rely more on people to effectively communicate. He'll have to pause and think a bit deeper to figure out new ways to express old phrases. Le va ser mas dificil performing basic functions, like snapping a picture with his cellphone. Maybe those extra seconds of fumbling will help him rethink his initial instinct, decide it's not worth it. Maybe he'll keep being the same prick, but at least now he's perpetually muted. The world gets a break.

Sandy is still gone. Me and Tomas are forever vilomahs. The world will continue turning with people like Gabe on it. One silenced, thumbless prick avenged does not heal the world, but it heals us five. Selfishly, that brings me comfort and peace.

I've brought peace of mind to Tomas, Bernardo, Bailey, and Janaina. My misfit family born of tragedy, thriving through violence, sharing a pact we'll carry in our stomachs. An ulcer tattooed from loyalty and vengeance. Thicker than water. How Hispanic mother of me.

Gabe lies unconscious in the car, stars above him twinkling, one moment brightening, the next dimming, as if singing him to sleep. It's a serene image; more than he deserves. How Hispanic vilomah of me.

"We've done good," I say as the town car carries us back home.

Everyone stays quiet.

Gabe Acevedo

He wakes up in the middle of somewhere. Outside, wrapped in a tight blanket moist with dew. What the fuck? Did he say that or think it?

He scrambles to wiggle from out the blanket but can't get a good grip. Is he tied down?

"What the fuck?" he says but doesn't say. Something's lodged in his mouth, wiggling like a fat, wet slug. It lays an acrid taste of iron. He swallows against it and chokes. He crunches up to sitting position, coughing up blood and saliva, sticking his tongue out to hock. A stub hits the roof of his mouth. "Help," he yells. But grunts. Against his effort, just a grunt.

"Fuck." He stands to yank the blanket off him but can't get a grip. What the fuck kind of muscle relaxant was his drink laced with? The blanket falls from around his body. His hands aren't tied. Why's he having so much trouble. . .

They're his hands but not. Thumbs gone off each of them. Seeing the missing digits registers a wave of pain over his four-fingered palms. He screams. Not a scream; a grunt he choke-swallows. He pulls his phone from his left pocket. It drops on the floor. The screen brightens on a message in large, black bold letters: **MY NAME IS GABRIEL ACEVEDO. I'VE DONE SOME BAD SHIT**. He kneels and bends closer to the ground to read it.

"Help!" he screams again but can't. It turns into a laugh. Out loud or in his head? His heart beats faster than he can breathe. Parched, he swallows compulsively against a dry mouth. He runs to the river shore and laps up water that's the consistency of battery acid. Something shuffles around in his right pocket. A bottle of pills. His beating heart and aching hands call for numbness. He pops a couple of pills and laps up more water. The pills lodge in his throat. He screams for help. It's a grunt. The pills tuck cozily behind his Adam's apple. He swallows back against them but can't. His heart thumps against his chest. He laps up more water. His throat fills. He coughs, grunts, and chokes, bringing a hand to his neck. It slides off.

Without grip, voice, or air, he chokes behind a tongueless mouth. Grunts forever unheard. With darkness enveloping him, Gabe Acevedo thinks on the heaping-mass, freak carcass he's leaving behind and stops trying to survive.

Bailey, Bernardo, Janaina, Tomas, and Ximena

They share coffee on the balcony looking out over El Escambrón.

Tomas and Ximena live together but neither say they're back together. There's much more patience, understanding, love, and respect between them now, here in Puerto Rico. They left all their bad blood in Miami.

Ximena doesn't act anymore. She's still famous and loved across the island and Latin America, which helped her charity pick up steam in the year since the tragedy.

The Sandy Mangual Foundation helps those addicted to social media and brings attention to the psychological effects of constantly plugging in. Major artists and influencers are on board. The foundation raised millions in its first year, consistently attracting donors.

Bailey works as Ximena's full-time assistant with promises of eventually heading the organization.

Tomas's company, Isla Development, helped rebuild the island after a hurricane swept through and their pain went mostly ignored by the rest of the world. Bernardo is his head foreman. Tomas goes on and on about how he needs more people with his kind of drive, initiative, and ball-busting mouth.

Bailey and Bernardo share an apartment together in the same building. As friends. What more intimacy do they need than the secrets shared between them?

At first, news outlets called for blurbs. Gabe's story attracted international attention with its gory details but was eventually chalked up to a mob vendetta after he blackmailed the wrong victim. Distraught with his mangled state, Gabe Acevedo found it easier to exit existence than face it. The story was buried and forgotten weeks later as the world continued turning on its chaotic axis.

Despite that chaos, the quintet provides its own order. Whenever one's in trouble, the rest swoop in. No questions asked, no favors expected in return. If they're there for one another, who can be against them? Five misfits in a chaotic world that continues turning with and without them. Perhaps, even, because of them.